SARA'LEON

ANTHONY ROBSON

SARA'LEON

TATE PUBLISHING
AND ENTERPRISES, LLC

Published by Tate Publishing & Enterprises, LLC
127 E. Trade Center Terrace | Mustang, Oklahoma 73064 USA
1.888.361.9473 | www.tatepublishing.com

Tate Publishing is committed to excellence in the publishing industry. The company reflects the philosophy established by the founders, based on Psalm 68:11,
"The Lord gave the word and great was the company of those who published it."

Cover design by Rtor Maghuyop
Interior design by Honeylette Pino

Published in the United States of America

ISBN: 978-1-63418-886-9
Fiction / General
14.10.31

THE INSPIRATION SARA' LEON

Just as my first book titled *Earth Walk the Meaning*, a voice only I heard prompted me to write down what it said, so I did. As I was working on my first book, I took a quick break to look out my window at the cars in my apartment building parking lot. I heard something whisper closely behind my right ear. However, before I heard the voice, I felt my bedroom become heavy, as if something was approaching directly behind me.

I continued to look at the cars in the parking lot, even though I felt something standing behind me. What I felt in my room whispered, "Sara' Leon, chapter crime. Sara', I, high chief of the courts of the planet Adamen, sentences you to your doom, to reside on the planet Arcturus, third planet from the Earth's sun. Is there anything you wish to say, Ms. Leon?"

Furthermore, I don't want to lose the meaning of my message of my inspiration. I want to thank the voice and the world, for help changing my life dramatically. I never knew that I could really do much of anything, and I sometimes found myself having issues of concern toward my life. However, I learned to listen to my voice and love the world and the people living on it, so support the voice and enjoy its work, "The Queen of Kingdoms."

SARA', THE PURPOSE

Sara' is bold, beautiful, strong and in so many ways magnificent!

Sara' wants the world to know that her dominance is forthcoming to earth. I would like for everyone to enjoy Sara" Leon. However, Sara' is to deliver a message to all the women around the world. She is taking a stand for what's right—no longer will the sexes be separated by brute strength or male dominance. Sara' has arrived, bearing knowledge and wisdom for all of us, especially the women whom are oppressed by their superiors. She is here to correct the world and guide us all into a new generation—a generation of women who rightfully accept their strengths and weaknesses that will eventually consume us all, destroying our righteousness. Although throughout the book many will question Sara"s ruling over and over again because of the way she demands order and discipline. Be patient! "Why is it, that women can accept trials that burden their hearts, but as men the superior species, we cannot accept what, is and what will always be."

CONTENTS

PLANET ADAMEN!

Six light years from earth, life inhabits a planet, leaving mankind not alone in existence. The universe is large and for as long as mankind could count his very own existence, he has come to forcefully believe that he inhabits the universe alone. Adamen Is a planet which orbits a star only three times its size. However, the planet is surrounded by three unique moons in its part of the universe, making the beings of the planet advanced nocturnal residents.

The planet is beautiful and has many waterfalls and rivers, cities, and valleys. The planet also has presidential campaigns and protests. The beings of the planet Adamen are universal relatives of earthlings, and share the same bodily appearance and functions as Earth people.

The beings of Adamen are slightly larger than the humans of earth, due to their abnormal bone growth. The sun only brightens the sky of this planet for similar to four earth hours a day. Adamen has technology that exceeds earth by thousands of years. The people of Adamen are pale-skinned beings, and beautiful in the appearances of "GODS" and goddesses.

The people of Adamen are tall, slender creators. The women of the planet have long slanted eyes, and long, luxurious hair. The men of the planet are broad-chested and inches taller than the average women on their planet. Every being from Adamen is divinely built, meaning perfect health and physique touches every person on the planet.

Looking down into the planet, through the thick and rich-colored purple clouds of the night, there's an area of land where the people of the planet inhabit the streets, moving around similar to the way humans would at twelve o'clock in the evening earth time. However, the difference was that it's nighttime on Adamen for the nocturnal beings.

Social conflict was building up on Adamen, For the female population. Women on the planet were harassed from their male counterparts, and were even raped and killed in high numbers just for merely being women. The males of the planet naturally began to notice that the women had begun to severely outnumber them. The outnumbering caused differences to flare on the planet and the female population was under heavy attack from a new and powerful ruler who wished to suppress the women of his planet. The new ruler believed that all women should have curfews and planned parenting and any women who wishes to not register for pregnancy and wishes to have illegal children will be publicly executed. Education had been removed from public places and women were not allowed to study alongside the males of their planet, a new rule which was placed from the new ruler.

The new ruler believed that women were wicked and Uncontrollable creatures that must experience dominance over them. "The male population numbers have diminished over the last decade on the planet, due to a discovery of a new gene called the "Celsius gene, giving women the ability to dictate their sex of birth", the ruler of Adamen addressed his people. The ruler of Adamen had publicly chosen further, to deliver a second message to the people of his planet. "*Adamanians,* I your ruler will decide which percentage of women will have male or female pregnancies.

Men, women lack respect for our planet and their peers and one day they will grow to love each other and exclude you from your world and into the abyss of no existence. All the males of Adamen will come to be known as extinct creatures.

During this, the ruler and his advisers planned a public notification of the adversities, that all women on his planet must face. Thousands of Adamen men and women swarmed the streets of their capital city to witness the day that all women must be dominated for the sake of their world. The new ruler's advisors ironically consisted of the female gender who thought it appropriate to suppress their fellow sisters of nature. The ruler and his advisers stood high off the ground of the capital, on top of a special platform made for powerful people and public elections, which were similar to earth during their presidential elections.

The people of Adamen had what we on earth would call supernatural powers, they were able to move at tremendous speeds and move objects, through pyhcothynises. Teleportation was capable of the people as well, but prohibited on the planet Adamen. However, in anticipation of a public outcry that could have potentially caused a rebellion, nothing happened. Shortly after the new ruler delivered his speech, thousands of men filled the streets clapping and cheering their ruler's decision to oppress the women species. The women standing next to the men in the streets held their heads down in disbelief and resentment of the new ruler, and understanding that they will undoubtedly have to bear new adversities that would shape the history of their planet.

The men of Adamen stood seven feet tall and the average height of the women is six feet. After the speech was delivered to the people, the men standing in the crowd seemingly towered above the women pride-fully. The women turned and left the open streets headed for their homes quickly as possible, because of the new curfew that was immediately placed into effect. Hundreds of women disappeared simultaneously from the streets. The women were saddened from their new ruler's decision. The streets once full of people gathered around, were now barren and desolate.

However, one female figure stayed standing amongst the men in the open streets. She was not intimidated by her male counterparts as she turned and walked away slowly, defying the new order on her planet. The women grew up an orphan on her planet and grew up on the hard streets of Adamen. Her mother and younger sister were murdered from strange men, seeking to locate her father whom was a scientist of her planet. The women swore to never let her environment become unstable. However, after the ruler of Adamen finished addressing the crowd, he was ushered away by his protective entourage to safety. The streets in the capital city were empty of all female presence, and only Adamen males stood openly in the streets as they appeared happy to have taken their planet back from the women of their world.

The new ruler and his team of thirty-six people went to eat dinner and celebrate his victory over his imposers, the women of his planet. However, his every move was closely monitored from a presence which will become the judge of his last night alive. The ruler of Adamen drank heavily and enjoyed his company and the respect they showed him. He loved his authority. The female members of his team also enjoyed the advantage over their fellow sisters of nature, as they looked down on the female waiters who served them and their new ruler and companions. "You women should feel privileged to serve us considering your new curfew," a female member of the ruler, mentioned to one her hostess.

Photos were taken of the ruler and his companions from the presence that monitored them closely. Shortly after dinner was over for the ruler and his teammates, security eased up a bit as they became relaxed. Each companion of the new ruler chose to go their individual way, and head home to their family's and loved ones.

The capital city of Adamen was dark and had many large shadows walking the streets drunken from celebration of the curfew and dominance over women, while the women remained home with their children, worried of the new adversities they must face from their new world. Other women around the planet were beaten by their drunk husbands, whom came home late from celebrating of the adversities for women. A large majority of Adamen men, overly took the new ruler's decision as choices to make women slaves, while other Adamen males beat their wives for sport.

Many women prayed to the creator of their world before going to bed, asking their creator to be with them through the uncertainties of this harsh and cruel time. Many

Adamen men laid drunken on the floors of their homes, or wherever their drunken bodies allowed them to rest, many of the men did not make it home. However, the night had gone quickly and daybreak had soon arrived, allowing daytime creatures of their planet to roam loosely. There were different daytime animals similar to earth; there were animals appearing like birds, except the animals had four wings instead of two. Also, a few Adamenians, females and males alike, walked the streets taking advantage of daytime shopping hours, the day time shoppers wanted to avoid any outbreak on the streets from events last night.

Adamenians who walked the street during the day stood motionless in their early daytime grocery stores and shopping centers, as they watched television monitors of the tragic deaths of the ruler and his teammates. Good day Adamanians, we have a tragic occurrence that has impacted the entire planet this morning, the new ruler "HIBA" and his team of advisers, were all brutally murder and the killer were abouts, are unknown. The males of the planet screamed angrily and tore pieces of their clothes from their bodies, and the women hurried and rushed themselves back to the safety of their homes.

No female gender wanted to be out an on the streets that morning, after hearing how the ruler "HIBA" was slain. Women feared that they would be singled out and murdered because women already out numbered men on Adamen, by four to one ratio and they wished not to be hunted, because of their gender.

However, three weeks later, the curfew and many things that the newly deceased ruler put into place, remained standing as law around the planet. However, the individual responsible for the deaths of the ruler and his board of members, had been apprehended and faces a set day to stand trial before jurors of their peers. Outside a courthouse, many women and men alike stood to witness a new day once again in their planet's history. The people wanted to see the arrival of the accused person responsible for saving or cursing their world, consequently from murdering the now dead ruler.

A single person was brought from a special vehicle escorted by officials in front of the crowded courthouse. The person had some sort of jacket thrown across its head, trying to conceal a clear image from the media or trying to prevent any successful assassination attempts from any angry individuals.

The murderer was pushed through the noisy and confused crowds of people. Noticing, the women of the crowds did not make any sound. They were exhausted mentally. However, the males of the planet spat on the accused killer and shouted filthy language at the person.

The killer of the new ruler stood before many courtroom judges and public safety advisers. The court was extremely packed and unbarring with loud noises. The jacket was pulled from the head of the person accused of killing thirty-six important man and women, and the courtroom grew deadly silent.

CRIME!

"As head official, I sentence the guilty to the term of eternity to reside on the planet Arcturus, third planet from the sun. Sara', you have been found guilty by your peers of the crimes of murder of many important Adamen, man and women. Sara', as high chief official Ruddick of the courts, of planet Adamen, I banish you to your death Ms. Leon, is there anything you wish to speak?"

Sara' was heavily guarded by nine large nocturnal males, as she stood before a podium of courtroom officials. Sara' attempts no response of any regarding her banishment from her home planet. Two of the nine guards surrounding Sara' held each of her arms firmly, and the remaining seven guards stood directly behind Sara', ready for anything that could possibly go wrong.

Everyone present feared the murderous harlot and dared not to give her long periods of visual eye contact. Sara' deeply glanced in the direction of the courtroom jurors, catching eye contact with a woman juror from her planet.

The juror swiftly tried to turn from Sara"s path. However, the woman couldn't remove the invisible lock that had hold of her from killer. The judge looked at Sara' staring at the juror box and noticed nothing oddly or unfamiliarly wrong, and finished addressing Ms. Leon.

The woman juror begins to whimper loud enough to be heard from the people sitting near her. The juror box was filled with eighteen men and two women jurors. Sara"s guilty verdict was a unanimous decision that only took merely a few minutes. The woman Sara' possessed bled from her eyes and moved her head from side to side slowly.

A large male juror, sitting next to the women juror, was the first to notice the bleeding woman, and began to stand up pointing toward Sara', screaming, "She wants to kill again."

All jurors rose to their feet, running and jumping from the juror box, in fear of Sara'. The male guards all grabbed hold of Ms. Leon and slammed her on her back on the courtroom floor, forcing her to look up at the ceiling of the large dark courtroom.

More armed guards rush inside the courtroom, making sure that everyone present left the room protected and unharmed from Sara"s harmful intent. People vacated the courtroom panicked and confused of why their emergency evacuation was so seriously necessary. The judge continued to speak with great authority to Sara' regarding her banishment. However, the judge's words went in vane from all the commotion that had taken place. Sara' looked up at the roof of the courtroom and focused on the large monitors on the court room ceiling that displayed her crimes.

The monitors displayed many dead Adamenians, male and female alike, dead from large projectile wounds to the head execution style on the floors of their homes and apartments. Furthermore, some of the victims were killed in front of family and loved ones. There were a total of thirty six-victims murdered. Some of the victim were pulled apart from their limbs and heads. Ten of the thirty-six were women. The women's arms and hands were tied behind their backs, with their heads decapitated from their bodies.

Sara' never flinched a muscle from being slammed to the floor of the courtroom. However, she zeroed her attention on the courtroom monitors. Sara' noticed her reflection through the glass of the monitor's lenses, as she widened up her eyes trying to access any possible escape routes through the glare of the lenses. Sara' noticed many people running wildly throughout the courtroom. The guards continued to lie on top of Sara', as the guards breathed heavily. Each was equipped with emergency combat gear. They each wore bulletproof helmets with purple protective lenses.

All six guards placed some part of their bodies on top of Sara' Leon, pinning her down on the floor. Sara' now lay on her back in an X position, with a guard lying across each of her arms. Sara' turned her head, looking into the eye of the guard holding down her left arm, making the larger male guard urinate through his uniform. The protective glass on the guard's helmets was capable of withstanding high-caliber weapon fire at close range. However, somehow Sara' stimulated the glass and caused its temperature to rise, making the solid material melt.

The guard, frightened, immediately removed himself from Sara''s left arm. The guard frantically started crawling away from Sara' as he feared her capabilities. Sara' continued to watch the fleeing male guard, while the remaining five occupied spaces on her body. The fleeing guard was levitated across the courtroom and thrown into the high official addressing Sara', him with tremendous force, causing both the guard and the judge to be knocked into a neighboring courtroom.

The remaining guards, filled with great fear, removed themselves cautiously from Ms. Leon's body. The guards all feared eye contact so they kept their eyes to the ground and instinctively understood the exit points out the courtroom as they placed their arms and hands behind their backs, feeling for courtroom chairs and benches not to fall over, as they attempted to flee for their lives. Ms. Leon slowly got up from the courtroom floor and turned toward the remaining officials on the podium. The officials were all males who seemingly predicted that death was now in their futures, and they understood they would not exit the courtroom alive.

Many people exited the once-packed courtroom screaming and jumping over others and courtroom furniture, desperately not wanting to be around the female murderer. The courtroom suddenly became silent. All the male officials standing on the podium held their hands together with their fingers intertwined and locked together submissively, in front of Ms. Leon. Some officials dropped to their knees and hid themselves under the large podium, praying to their creator. Other official's bled from their eyes, notifying Sara' that she doesn't have to murder once again and that killing them will not solve anything.

There were a total of ten judges remaining, four of them hiding underneath the wooded podium and five standing before Sara', pleading that murder is meaningless on the planet Adamen. One of the five judges took a leadership position amongst the remaining five officials and tried to reason with Ms. Leon, asking for their safe release. Sara' approached the pleading official silently.

Sara' reached a height of six feet and she was dangerously beautiful to many lookers. The male officials, however, fearful of Sara', couldn't help not to overlook her beauty. The leading judge silenced himself and continued to be brave before the approaching woman. Sara' reached out her arm and hand, inviting the judge closer. The judge procrastinated her invitation, but allowed his hand to make physical contact with hers.

They both touched hands and immediately the court room official began to turn dark orange, the same color as lava from Earth's volcanoes. The judge's arm turned to ashes and began to fall to the floor. The judge looked at his arm and hand as his entire limb fell from his body. The other officials started begging Ms. Leon for mercy. The leading official had completely turned to ashes and now fell on top of the podium floor.

Sara' looked from right to left in all the judges' direction. Sara' paused and looked at the floor, appearing to be deep in thought before turning completely around, facing the courtroom entry and exit doors. A group of patient and silent guards knelt down on one knee, with their assault weapons pointed at Sara', ready for her death. Sara' took one step in the guards' direction and the trained unit opened fire, with gun lamps that shot out multiple light cylinders the size of a box of raisins. Each light cylinder projected five thousand watts of light per-hundred feet, which blinded Sara', causing her to cover her eyes and fall to her knees.

The guards all had protective uniform equipment, which permitted them to withstand the wattage of their gun lamps.

Once the nocturnal woman fell to her knees, a specific group of staff shot the blinded Sara' with specialized darts that contained preset doses of medication. Sara' fell to her side from the strong medication. She stared in their direction. However, Sara''s eyes were burned from the bright lights and only boldly stares at the guards from blindness.

The drugs were designed to shut the brain down first, second the heart and lungs also shut down, putting the body into a medically induced coma. Sara' was now safe to be approached. Special medical examiners placed Sara' on her back and placed her hands down her side, and turned her neck to the right, clearing clothing from a large area of Ms. Leon's neck for the purpose of delivering the final dose of medication needed for her sedation.

A chief medical examiner stood over Sara' with a very long pole, about three feet in length, which supported a forty-nine gram cylinder attached on the end which would deliver the final dose of the medication. Sara''s body started to quiver, and she lost all sense of awareness. Sara''s last vision before she was medically induced was a very large male sticking a large rod into the side of her neck.

DETOUR!

The courtroom smelled of burned flesh hair and clothing. The heat from the lamp guns' light projectors were intense, burning the furniture in the courtroom. Ms. Leon was lying on the floor, exhaling and inhaling extremely heavily due to her sedation. People reentered the courtroom, curious to look at the murderer's limp body.

Sara' had many people standing over her, almost admiring her, as she lay unconscious and unaware of them. Armed guards and medical examiners tried their best to barricade Sara''s body from the onlookers. They built a shield of bodies around her unconscious frame. Further observing the courtroom, the judges hiding behind the large podium began to rise from their hiding spots, feeling that they were safe to show themselves once again now that Sara' was successfully put down.

The chief medical examiner who delivered the final dose needed to make certain Sara' was incapable of being a potential threat to anyone else. He pulled a pager from his red uniform pocket and pushed the yellow button on top of the device. The pager was a part of an emergency detour team that was in charge of overseeing Ms. Leon's departure from the planet. Six men rushed in the courtroom pushing a gurney meant to carry away Sara'. The six men were responding to the page they received.

The guards and others protecting Sara''s body from the onlookers were forced out of the way by the six men. Medical examiners followed closely, observing the six men's every move, as they positioned themselves around Sara''s body. Each of the men pushing the gurney towered over Sara', before picking her limp body and placing it on the wheel-operated gurney.

People gazed upon the woman murderer as she lay across her portable medical bed, fully unconscious of her surroundings. Wet black towels were placed over her eyes to protect her burned retinas from further damage. Several straps have also been placed across Sara''s body, to prevent any possible threat or attack from her. The gurney men stood on the left and right sides of the medical bed, three on each side. The men have been signaled to push the bed from the courtroom to their trained practice location.

Dozens of people moved themselves out the path of the men pushing Sara''s medical bed. The men pushed Sara' through the smoking and partially burning courtroom, past many wounded and ill people standing in the door way of the courtroom while they held themselves and others. However, the six men determinedly pushed past the onlookers.

Sara' was pushed out the doors of the courtroom and headed to the left side of the hallway, headed further down the long walkway of the courthouse. There were many doors down the long hallway and many Adamenians stuck some part of their bodies out the doors of the courthouse. Fifteen armed guards followed closely behind the six men pushing Sara' down the hallways of the courthouse. After passing several groups of Adamenians, the guards escorting Sara' made a sharp right and another immediate right, causing the guards to bump into each one another.

Sara' entered into a very large room that transformed into an emergency evacuation elevator. The medical bed which Sara''s body occupied entered the motion-room completely now. The six men marched in the room in uniform order, creating a safe functional operation of the delivery of Sara' to her first rendezvous. The six men did an about face.

Twelve armed guards crowded outside the emergency room, protecting the staff that participated in the evacuation. The guards were also there to prevent any escape attempts from persons seeking to rescue Sara'. Six guards faced inside the room and the remaining six guards turned and faced the outside hallway on high alert from threats. The medical men faced the guards and gave them a signal to back away from the entrance of the room.

Doors began to shut close on the guards and slightly bumped into the tip of one of the guard's foot. The guard quickly looked down at his foot and backed away from the moving room.

Adamenians were curiously searching down the hallways of the courthouse for Sara' and the group who evacuated her so quickly down the hallways. The six guards who faced the outside hallway raised their weapons at the approaching group of people.

Suddenly, the room started to move and descend below the guards and approaching crowd outside the room. Six of the guards all pushed each other from the small window of the emergency room as they each needed to see the room move. The guards now took turns as they tapped each other on the shoulders so they can look at Sara' for the last time.

Examiners looked up at the feet of the guards outside the room from the crack under the door. Sara' remained deeply in sleep inside her sedated coma, as one of the six examiners stared at Sara''s chest area, making sure that she did not stop breathing. The room sank further below to a location only known to the computer installed inside the room's brain. The six examiners have only practiced going up and down the moving room. However, the six men have never exited the room below the negative floors of the courthouse, making their mission transferring Sara''s body unpredictable.

The room had reached depths that exceeded what the six examiners experienced and they expressed movements of panic. The large white letters above the door read negative twenty ninth floor, and the group had never before gone negative floors. The deepness of Sara''s departure causes the men's ears to clog up from the pressure of being so deep below ground level. The room stopped moving at thirty-three.

The room completely stopped its movement, and the doors started to open themselves. The doors opened entirely, and there stood a very tall woman and a man, waiting for Sara' to be delivered to them so that they may dress her body out for departure to the crippling planet Arcturus, third planet from the planet earth's sun. Sara' was a nocturnal being and naturally adapts to a dark climate. Jupiter was much closer to the sun than Sara' could ever have imagined. The temperature on the planet was over nine thousand degrees Celsius on any given day and the planet had no oceans. However, there was water on the planet but it remained below ground.

The large men and women who received Sara"s body now pulled the medical bed through the entrance of the moving room. The bed was pulled from the entrance of the room, and the man and woman both walked on each side of the bed, further leading the unconscious Ms. Leon down a generated lighted hallway to her final destination. The light from the moving room that delivered Sara' below ground grew dim as it disappeared from view as the doors closed shut delivering the six examiners back above ground to a positive level of the court building.

Sara' was walked further down the hallway into a room with an electronic chute. The electric chute was designed to carry the gurney to a pod where Sara"s body will be placed in. Once Sara' was placed inside the pod, she will be further carried to a ship for space travel. Sara' now headed toward her pod and reached the pod in under twenty seconds.

The pod opened up, and the murderer was placed safely inside the capsule. The capsule closed after her body was placed inside. Everything turned black. The pod further proceeded on course toward the ship for departure. The pod was scanned from medical equipment designed to check the capsule/pod for durability issues along its journey down the electric chute.

Several machines scanned codes inscribed into the metal of the pod/capsule. The machines scanned for weight, length, and most importantly durability for its space travel. The capsule ran its course through what appeared to be an underground warehouse, which was full of machines. No physical presence operated this apparent facility room. The room was remotely operated by men viewing monitors.

Conveyor belts proceeded throughout the length of the underground building and further out through the side of the structure. The conveyor belts were also known as transportation belts. These carried Sara' to her destination. Everything was extremely black inside the pod/capsule and there was nothing to see. However, Sara' could be heard breathing lowly inside the quiet capsule.

Different movements were felt as the pod/capsule moved closer in the direction of the ship. The arrival time with the spaceship was under two minutes. The capsule travelled over thirty stories underground, heading through its last cycle before it entered the space ship now about sixty seconds away. The underground lighting, was fluorescent red flashing lights.

The final destination of the pod/capsule was reached, and the pod entered a small entranceway that appeared to be going outside to enter the rear of Sara''s ship. The pod/capsule traveled outside and entered the rear of the spaceship. However, the outside of the ship was not visible and only the inside of the ship was available for viewing. There were many different colored lights that occupied the ship's control panel. The pod now was secure and placed in the middle of the craft and locked in placed by motion sensors that notified the ship main computer, making sure the capsule was firmly located in its proper position.

Many officials watched from multiple monitors as Sara' was loaded into the ship headed for her coordinates to the dangerous planet Arcturus? The rear of the ships doors close shut and the inside of the craft darkens from many of the control panel lights flickering on and off, as the computerized ship prepare for its forty year travel to the murderous inhabited planet Arcturus. The outside of Sara"s ship began to light up the ground's surface surrounding the craft. The jet boosters located on the bottom of the ship, blew dust and small insects from the ground as the ship built strength for the long flight ahead.

Looking through the monitors from the courthouse and the homes of many important men and women, everyone witnessed Sara' begin her departure from their planet. Many people celebrated and others mourned the deaths of lost and dead relatives that came across Sara"s path of destruction. Also, small girls and boys cried for their parents who have been lost forever, due to the murders that will never be forgotten from their young minds.

The ship gently left the ground and rose higher into the planet's atmosphere. A cloud of the purest white smoke followed close behind the ship, making the cameras attached to the spaceship temporally blinded from the thick clouds of heated air and smoke. The ship reached a height of two kilometers which was a little more than a mile from the ground. The monitors which first displayed Sara"s departure came to focus clearly, as the thick clouds of smoke followed far behind the ship, now that the ship v higher into the atmosphere.

The ship continued to quickly gain kilometer footage, as the ship reached higher and higher for black space. It took the spaceship roughly three kilometers before the craft could fully reach open space. Reaching open space, the craft suddenly stopped all motion, before it reached speeds of more than seventeen thousand miles an hour. The ship's home quickly becomes ever so small as Sara' left her home for eternity. The ship was scheduled to reach its destination in forty-eight earth hours.

Banished forever, Sara' left her home for good, as she headed for Arcturus. The ship approached an entirely white planet. The planet had no air on it, and it looked like a deserted battlefield. Sara"s spaceship quickly passed more than half the distance of the white planet in merely minutes. Looking out the right side of the spacecraft, there was a green planet with thick white clouds that choked its planet's atmosphere with carbon dioxide and heated air.

Leaving the white and green planets' space zone, there was a noticeable absence of stars that made this area of space creepy. The black spot of space that surrounded Sara"s ship will take the ship over four hours before any light at all will brighten up the air of space. There is much space trash that fluttered around in black space, making safe travel through space an uncertainty. Many small space rocks hit the ship, and some even knocked dents into its tough metal.

Everything was completely black in space except for the lights of the control panel of Sara"s ship, which glowed softly into space. However, the lights were not capable of making the ship visible so the craft remained invisible. There were many strong gravitational pulls inside of this black area, the craft motioned *un*controllably, setting off different alarms throughout the spaceship.

Traveling through space effortlessly, the black spot revealed signs of promise as there appeared to be millions of stars up ahead. The craft continuously moved at tremendous speeds, causing the empty space between blackness and the stars ahead to lessen. Alarms sounded off loudly throughout the ship. However, these groups of alarms were different than the last alarms. Large comets rocked past the ship, causing the craft to rise and lower itself at different altitudes needed in order to avoid any and all collisions.

The large comets looked like large shadows moving quickly past the spaceship, Sara"s capsule slightly moved inside her ship, causing the hydraulics supporting the craft to release pressurized gases. Looking back upon space, the ship will reconnect back with a bright place amongst the stars in the galaxy's sky. The black spot was over as other planets and stars were in open window view of Sara"s ship. A bright star is picked up by the ship's computer.

The star was electronically identified as East. The star was known for being the brightest of its kind in the Milky Way system. The star East is under a half of an earth day from arrival with Sara' and her craft. The planet Arcturus was much closer than the star East and was not presently in view at the moment. The ship had picked up on a space storm and increased its speed as the computerized craft tried to best the storm ahead of it.

Sara"s ship had reached a maximum speed of thirty-five thousand earth miles an hour. Thousands of small space rocks hit the front and sides of the ship, creating no threat to the craft. The planet of arrival for the Unconscious murderer had come into fiery red view. The planet was hundreds of times larger than earth and its color was fiery red. The ship desperately tried to maneuver through the potentially hazardous storm. The craft had just entered Arcturus's space zone and tried hard to resist the strong gravitational pull that the planet possessed.

However, the storm sought out the craft by assaulting the ship once again, causing more space rocks to hit the ship, this time creating tennis ball-sized holes in the ship that created vacuum problems. Small space rocks punctured the strong material of the craft, hitting where Sara"s limp body lay. More rocks hit, aggressively assaulting the ship entering inside it. The storm caused major damage to the ship's control panels.

The ship traveled alone through space and the deadly storm that battered the craft, the control panel light flashed and the ship's coordinates have been redirected from the damage of the storm and now the craft verse left and headed further east of the star called East, and headed destined to crash into the much smaller blue, green, and white clouded planet called Earth.

CRASH!

Memorial Day weekend, the weather was excellent and the sky was full of blue with no clouds. Families around the country were celebrating their independence on this special day. Parents were also attending their children's sports ball games, through electronic monitor sun shades while grocery shopping at their local food stores. The images through the sun shades were 360-degree images of the children attending their games. The year of date is 2028, and people at this present time moved very swiftly because of world advancements. The motorcycle has been replaced with flying electric bikes, which were capable of having a maximum speed of 363 miles an hour. The bikes also were capable of a maximum height of 310 feet. However, the legal street height was twenty feet.

Life for earth had really began to evolve. Grocery stores have no cashiers, people have electronic credit chip implants which obtained who an individual and what his or her social rankings were and what an individual finances were. A crash had taken place in the city of Sana Monique, California, off the coastline of the city's beach.

Fireworks were legal again and people were enjoying the action of the coastline of the beach. The beach was extremely crowded this day due to the carnival having their main attraction. The main attraction was the man who will swim with tiger sharks while they feed. There were three sharks inside of a see-through aquarium, the three sharks were each over eighteen feet in length.

Meanwhile, children chased each other up and down the coast of the beach, laughing and playing. Also, the beach was full of dog owners who were enjoying the beach themselves. The owners had their dogs performing several tricks such as catching Frisbees and tugging ropes. The ocean water was aggressive off the coastline of the beach. The water was aggressive, caused by an underwater current, which in all, allowed fish called tuna axes passage so the animals could reach open water swiftly. However, surfers also benefited from the aggressive waves caused from the underwater current.

The time was 2:00 p.m. and the weather was 85 degrees, People from all around the Los Angeles county and country included have traveled tens and thousands of miles, to reach the ocean water for the purpose of watching the fireworks show. The parking lot of the beach was full of electric bikes, and jet-powered cars that were even quicker than the bikes. The carnival's main attraction was ready for their big performance—the man who will swim with feeding tiger sharks.

A man holding an electric blow horn announced that Henry the Shark Beast was ready to swim with the man-eating killers. The man named Henry eagerly dove into the tank, and instantly headed for the bottom. The sharks swam above the man, while other persons from the carnival fed chunks of frozen horse meat to the animals. Once the sharks were full, which didn't take long, considering the sharks were taking thirty-pound mouthfuls of horse flesh inside one bit. Henry began to control his buoyancy, and made his way up from the bottom of the aquarium while the sharks swam in circles, drunk from overfeeding. People were cheering and praising Henry very loudly as he made his way up from the bottom of the tank safely, when a very loud whistling sound interrupted everyone on the entire beach.

The sound appeared to come from up in the sky, past the sun. The whistle was getting louder and more annoying each second, causing people's noses to bleed and their eardrums to burst. People began running in all directions. The people who were in the water started to swim back to shore. They were afraid also because they heard the loud whistle through the splashing water. People were swimming as fast as possible, scratching the sand with their hands and feet once they met the joint between water and land.

Above in the sky, the sound was affiliated with an alien craft breaking through the earth's atmosphere. The craft was shiny, like stainless steel, and it looked similar to the ship from Star Trek, called *Akira*. The craft was approaching the beach at what appeared to be hundreds of thousands of miles an hour. People who were in the parking lot ran toward the sound, trying to find the source of the commotion.

The people who where on the beach were screaming for their lives as the craft approached.

The alien spaceship was moving so gracefully through the earth's atmosphere as people continued screaming. The craft was approaching at the speed of what appeared to be a football field every two seconds. People from the beach and parking lot jumped in their cars and on their electric bikes and sped off trying to avoid the ship which wanted to crash into the edge of the beach front.

Many other people through the beach on this day ran as fast as possible also. However, the craft attacked the beach with tremendous force, causing several major populated cities having to endure without electricity or different kinds of utilities. Also, many innocent people were killed from the impact of the ship crashing into the beach. The ship dug itself deep into the beach, as it quickly tried heading toward the parking lot. People could not run fast enough to escape the ship's path. Some people's internal organs were turned into liquid jelly, and that was not clearly understood why. The ship headed toward the parking lot crashing into a small mountain, which separated the parking lot from the beach.

Smoke, sand, large rocks, and debris traveled everywhere. The ship was broken into pieces and embedded into the beach and parking lot divider. The ship's nose locked into the ground like an anchor of a ship, causing the remainder of the craft to flip over itself. People ran and screamed for miles around. Helicopters started to fill the sky. They were flying frantically, unable to focus on multiple areas of destruction caused by the crash.

People from the beach who remained in the parking lot elevated their bikes and cars to their maximum flying heights, escaping most of the back blast from the unidentified object that have just crashed into the beach of Santa Monica, California. The smoke from the wreck began to clear, and there were trails of blood and body parts amongst the beach. The smoke totally cleared and screaming people from around the beach were now starting to calm down and head toward the unidentified object that had killed so many innocent people.

People from the beach left the peer and also followed the other crowds in the direction to the ship. The bikes and cars descended down toward the crashed ship. The bikes and cars hovered over the spaceship, trying to seek better view points, when suddenly emergency sirens filled the air, furthering the commotion. Hundreds of people now surrounded the ship taking pictures with their cell phones and electric sun shades cameras. Sigils, pelicans, and many other large birds from the beach were eating human body parts which were scattered along the crash site.

Police helicopters arrived before any emergency vehicles. Police officers began to jump out of their helicopters in an attempt to control the large crowd. There were three police helicopters in total, each having six men. The police officers were equipped with fuel-powered jet packs. The officers each jumped head first toward the crowd, surrounding the ship. Hundreds of people continued their approach toward the wrecked ship also. However, they were weary with fear and full of inquiry.

The police jumpers flipped themselves upright yards before making contact with land and continued to fall toward the beach and crowd. The officers accelerated their packs to their maximum power to slow down the speed of their landing. Some officers headed immediately toward the crowd surrounding the ship, and other officers remained airborne, directing the electric bikes and cars hovering above the ship back toward the parking lot, for public safety.

Television cameras also hovered above the crowds on the beach and officers causing the sky to darken and blocking the sun periodically with their commercial helicopters. The police officers began to lower themselves on the beach, pushing the crowd out of the way, by forced air being accelerated out the back of their fuel-powered jet packs. People covered their heads and faces and began to scream louder from the apparent pain from the air of the officers' jet packs.

All officers landed in sync with one another, creating a chain of officers. The officers immediately gained dominance over the crowd, pushing the crowd back while looking at the ship, amazed and scared of not being able to predict what will happen next. People from the crowd yelled and screamed in no particular language, they were just screaming and scared because the scene on the beach was a tragedy, of this special day in America!

Suddenly breaking through the air and sound barrier, came the sound of more emergency vehicles. City ambulance, and Sana Monica coroner's trucks arrived also. The coroner trucks were there to collect the scattered parts. Both trucks floated across the sand of the beach. However, the vehicles did not blow sand every place as expected. The trucks were designed to vacuum up the sand and blow it out of the back of the vehicle, evenly toward the ground.

Each city employee arrived and immediately attacked their task at hand, securing the crash site. Wounded and dead people lay scattered amongst the ground, mentally or physically broken and shaken from the crash. Police officers were beginning to lose footing with the aggressive crowd. The crowd wanted to attack the burning craft, for killing friends and loved ones. Sana Monica SWAT arrived to assist the police department covering the wreckage. Looking out toward the ocean, in the horizon, there were military vessels appearing.

Back on the beach, the ship began to burn more intensely suddenly. The ship's metal began to burn, transforming into liquid metal form, puttying the ground. Officers and crowd members alike looked toward the ship forgetting their fight with one another. The ship rapidly began melting down, losing structural form. SWAT arrived on the scene to assist the police, and strengthen their barricade. They installed an electric barricade that would not allow the crowd beyond a certain amount of footage near the perimeter, guarding the ship.

The electric field perimeter temporarily paralyzed anyone touching the invisible field. The color of the new perimeter glowed florescent fire pink, and hundreds of people still remained surrounding the crash. However, the perimeter setup neatly organized the apparent disorder. Military ships surveillance teams take pictures of the crash site from more than a mile out to sea. Satellites from around the globe broke each country's boundaries and rushed toward that part of the world, seeking detail.

Satellites quickly gained mileage over the site, delivering world news to many different countries. There were eight satellites total hovering the solar system outside of America, over a city named Sana Monica, in the state of California. World leaders from around the world watched monitors focused on the crash. Top leaders of the United States immediately stopped what they were doing. Government helicopters and airplanes where quickly fueled, started, and ready for mission "Monica."

Electricity remained unoperational for the city of Sana Monica California and neighboring states from the crash, leaving much of the western part of the state unaware of the crash on the beach. Government and secret society people walked around the melting ship, praying and also asking questions to one another, concerned about an alien evasion. City coroner crews bagged partially eaten body parts and dead people beyond recognition off the sand of the beach.

The craft had melted down completely and the only thing that stood remaining, was a very large pill-shaped capsule. The capsule was twenty feet in length, and round enough for an African rhino to be placed inside. The pill-shaped object lay on the beach, surrounded by burning liquid metal. The capsule was brighter than any silver or aluminum on Earth.

The crowd ran back further voluntary, because the shine of the object blinded all onlookers. Helicopters and other machines hovering around the crash also were forced back, due to the brightness of the capsule. The shine beamed into space and was easily spotted by the satellites orbiting America's space zone. Television and police emergency personnel began to land their helicopters inside the beach parking lot because of the intense shine of the capsule.

The capsule began to make sounds of compressed air being released from it. Three holes located on each side of the pod released air, causing the capsule to shrink slightly in size. Special utility blankets were thrown on top of the pod from government officials in order to assure safety and also to dim the brightness of the capsule reflection. State leaders were directed out to sea off the coastline of the beach, headed for the military ships. The state leaders were instructed of a briefing concerning the ship, and its capsule and its removal from the beach.

The time was approximately 5:30 p.m. and different United States leaders also were en route to the military ships, late for the first briefings. Police officers, SWAT teams, and other structural forms pushed the crowds away from the crash, over three hundred yards away. The emergency perimeter automatically expanded itself every five minutes, allowing different crews the space they need to make sure the accident site was secure.

Coroner's crewmembers and biohazard teams sprayed the sand near the site, trying to kill any deadly hazards that should exist or evolve after the craft allowed different radiations to enter earth's atmosphere. The sun was becoming weaker as time passed considering the sun has been shining a third of the day. During the first briefing, a decision was made to allow the alien craft to be brought aboard the military vessel *Earl*, for further analysis.

A military helicopter was being fueled and prepared for departure from the military ship *Earl* to receive the craft and bring it aboard the ship. The military chopper was able to carry over thirty tons. The copter was equipped with cameras located on all sides of the military vehicle. Even the undercarriage had a camera. Police officers and swat laid down over twenty-six nylon straps preparing the capsule for its departure from the beach.

Captain Henry Robinson was the captain of *Earl*, from where the military helicopter was scheduled to leave and receive the product. The officers and SWAT had completed their task of laying down the straps for departure. Unknown to the SWAT or the officers, however, an early twentieth-century bulldozer had been brought in to grab and place the capsule on the nylon ropes carefully.

The bulldozer was brought in through the parking lot on the back of an "Air Rider." The air rider is the replacement of the eighteen wheeler. The eighteen wheeler and air rider are very similar in height and length; however, the Air Rider's engine was jet powered and also the truck was capable of 360-degree turns, on land or when airborne.

The officers and other personnel assisting the crash understood to exit the dozer's entry as it arrived from the parking lot of the beach. The dozer arrived and immediately picked up the capsule and gently placed it on the ropes which were placed down earlier by SWAT members moments ago. The military helicopter was being started from personnel aboard ship *Earl.*

There now was a race against time. The sun was beginning to set on the West Coast, and no one was willing to face the unexpectedness of nightfall. The captain of *Earl* released a team of trained Seals ahead of the helicopter, headed toward the beach. The Seals' job was for all eight members to secure the nylon connection tightly to the copter and the capsule when the military helicopter arrived over the target.

HOSPITAL!

The pod had been successfully connected and now hung airborne. The pod was followed by the trained Seals back to the ship. Other United States leaders have arrived from different parts of the country onto the ship, four at a time, from different government transportations. An emergency dismantle team of metal experts were ready for the arrival of the pod. Also, there were several metal x-ray machines aboard the ship.

X-rays of the object were necessary for further examination of the capsule, for more than safety reasons. Emergency personnel and other government agencies will continue to work the crash site, cleaning up all spills and containing any foreign substances. The pod's ETA was seven minutes out. Meanwhile, ship crewmembers scrambled for perfect unisons, and were honored of handling such a monstrous task. However, deck men tied ropes in place on the deck of the ship, for the helicopter anticipated perfect balanced landing.

The sun nearly was on its way out the door and the florescent light from the crash site could be seen far out from sea. The last government states leaders finally landed, and the helicopter transporting the capsule hovered almost directly over the ship. Every crewmember aboard *Earl* were ready to go and help things move forward smoothly.

It took seven minutes and twenty seconds for the capsule to arrive. Deck men waited each with one knee located on the surface of the deck of the ship and one arm reaching in the air for the slightest touch from the capsule. The helicopter pilot used his cameras to find the men directly underneath the helicopter. The capsule was lowered and the deck of the ship had many eyes watching. The sky was filled with news crews worldwide, and local channels. Television helicopters were ordered to back away from the military ship, and to keep a regulated distance.

The capsule was lowered completely on to a medical heavy-duty stretcher. Other crewmembers quickly pulled the capsule free from the deck men's location, and toward a special area of the ship. The deck men also quickly tied ropes under the belly of the helicopter, connecting the ropes and pulling the machine safely toward the deck of their ship.

Ten crewmembers, completely dressed in white, pushed the capsule through double doors located underneath the deck of the ship. A special area was set up for examination of the unidentified object. The men and the capsule were followed throughout the ship by military camera crews. Captain Henry Robinson escorted state and world leaders and many more important American leaders to a room that's strictly confidential, and only members will enter under the captain's supervision.

Military men and leaders, sat eagerly for the entrance of the pod. Inside the secure room, there was communication between leaders of the capsule being some type of nuclear weapon from outer space. There was even talk of the capsule being some type of charge device from the crash that would destroy the ship. Unexpectedly, a very important looking woman entered the room and asked everyone present to keep their voices underneath a whisper.

The room was bomb proof in case any uncertainties should occur. The room was located in the middle of the ship. The men respected the very important appearing woman which will come to be known as Ms. Thomas, the leaders quickly settled and sat down and focused straight ahead on the room before them. The men were behind eight-foot thick glass sheets for their protection. The capsule made its way through the ship's many elevators, when suddenly doors aggressively opened up straight ahead, and entered the capsule on the other side of the thick glass.

The capsule had fully made its way inside the examination room. The doors to the room were very large. It took two men to hold each door. The capsule entered the room covered inside an industrial blanket and nylon ropes. Next, the capsule was placed in the middle of the room. Government men immediately stood up, zeroing in on their target. The capsule was placed inside a very large stainless steel room, with multiple bright and colored lights.

The size of the actual capsule in live view was amazing to the leaders. The capsule stood there very large and similar to a torpedo. A military team of different metal experts entered the room, with different surgical tools attached to their waists. There stood a total of six men on each side of the foreign object. The men began to cut the ropes very carefully. Each of them reached up in the air in uniformity, grabbing down the industrial blanket from the capsule.

The blanket fell and caused the men to put their hands over their already protective helmet shades. The brightness of the capsule also caused the leaders behind the eight-foot thick glass slight discomfort. The lights in the examination room immediately turned yellow so that the bright shine of the capsule could be altered to protect the vision of everyone present. Also, noticeably the capsule was long and without scratches, considering what it had been through. The outer surface of the capsule seemed to have patterns all around its body.

The metal examiners scraped different parts of the pod/ capsule for samples, but only to have their scraping devices melt from making physical contact. The capsule apparently had no points of entry. The pod structure felt strength full. However, examining the capsule closely, it would seem the capsule served no purpose. The ship was equipped with many x-ray machine. One of the more powerful x-ray examining machines, were brought in the examining room.

The x-ray machine was more than capable of looking through materials that were eight feet thick. The machine entered the room, like supersized head phones. The x-ray machine easily slid perfectly over the pod. The metal examiners in the room stood back before the x-ray machine was turned on. The examiners all stood against the furthest wall, looking toward the government leaders in the next room behind the thick glass.

The x-ray machine was further designed to read four sides of the capsule at once. North, east, south, and west was examined inside of one reading. The light from the x-ray machine was fluorescent blue and when turned on and mixing with the bright yellow light of the examining room, the light surrounding the pod was aqua blue. The machine showed a picture through monitors located above the ceiling of the protected room. The machine began to read the difficult metal of the pod.

However, results were starting to show. The machine appeared to show some type of thick, liquid substance located on the inside of the pod. Everyone aboard the ship focused in on the results. The captain of the ship tightened up his fist and narrowed down at the pod from the examination room. Upon the examination, suddenly bone structure appeared to form. Leg-type limbs show on the monitors, and also a pelvis, similar to a woman's uterus bone.

Comprehending and understanding was clear that everyone present were starting to witness an extraterrestrial humanoid subject appearing before them all. Ribs came to focus and so did a head and an arm. The subject appeared feminine. The extra tissue surrounding the chest cavity suggested the results. The exclusive members allowed in the chambers were speechless! Everyone was deadly silent around the ship.

The figure was approximately six feet tall, and 150 pounds. The captain stood with his jaw hanging open and with one hand on top of his head. The examiners could not witness what the leaders were witnessing, they were not officially ranked important enough to view the pod contents from the x-ray machine. Instead, the examiners' purpose was to only extract fragments from the pod and hand them over to scientists aboard the ship. State leaders immediately got on their phones and made urgent calls to their higher ups.

During the reverse swipe of the x-ray machine, the pod begun to leak a Jell-o liquid from its sides. The liquid went unnoticed momentarily, until an examiner noticed the leak and pointed it out to his peers. Upon that information, the x-ray was put to a halt. All twelve examiners rushed the pods leak, but not to aid the leak, but anxiously eager to collect the leaking fluid from the pod. The pod surprisingly shot the fluid out forcefully through the holes of its sides, the holes were small shower type valves, which periodically popped in and out the pods body.

The pod began to expand itself, rising upward. Pressurized air was released and liquid wet the examining room floor. Examiners grabbed their heads and hit the floor. They've passed out from the pressurized air that released itself from the pod automatically. The pod began to open, flipping back its lid. The captain and other leaders glued themselves to the monitors.

The capsule had fully opened and revealed the image of a feminine humanoid woman. The woman was fully unclothed and had curly sandy black hair, animal appearing. Her skin appeared human like. Her facial structure also appeared human. However, her eyes were longer at their slits. The extraterrestrial woman's eyes were extremely black in their centers and white outer. The black of the woman's eyes were the size of quarters.

The humanoid woman also appeared to be resting in some type of medical sedation. Back inside the secure room, voice levels reached healthy above whisper level. Leaders were hugging each one another with faces of joy and hope of answers never answered toward life other than human. The president was notified immediately upon the results of information regarding the crash. The president ordered all information concerning mission "Monica" surrendered to his office only.

Examiners began to awaken trying to stand up from their hands and knees in the examining room. The examiners appeared aware of why they were unconscious and unwarily the examiners next began to remove their face masks, as if they were aware that the gas had been removed and designated into the emergency air shaft system, which was capable of removing all the air from the 30 X 50 foot room in under twenty seconds. The examiners gained full consciousness of their surroundings, and proceeded toward the capsule.

The examiners staggered toward the capsule to view its contents. All twelve men looked inside the pod at the humanoid and admired her beauty. The humanoid, physically and appearance wise, resembled an earth women; however, she is slightly tall for an earth woman, and her eyes are much larger. The humanoid woman's chest cavity inhaled and exhaled deeply and peacefully. Meanwhile, country leaders who were secured behind the protective glass demanded they be brought inside the room with the capsule and the humanoid woman.

The captain of *Earl* agreed with the leaders and immediately led them to the room, as the captain himself wanted to view the beautiful woman. Upon entering the room with the leaders, the captain was told from several of the leaders to have the examiners leave and exit with them and the pod. All the leaders and the captain included now hovered over the pod now that the examiners have left the room. Everyone stared at this woman and they couldn't believe what lay before their very own eyes. One of the leaders reached inside the pod and rubbed the woman's face, while other leaders spoke softly of how beautiful this creature of different intelligence truly was.

The special room which seated the country leaders now occupied many different officials and officers of the ship. They all wanted to view the woman, or life, from another planet. The captain and leaders all looked toward the protective room and the people inside of it, only to seem not bothered by their presence or about keeping something of this magnitude hidden from the crew personnel aboard the ship. The leaders understood how special a thing like this was. However, the captain interrupted the dozens of zero-in viewers of the capsule, by screaming, "Where are the medical examiners?"

Suddenly after hearing their captain's orders of them by asking for the medical examiners aboard the ship, they rushed to telephones located inside the room which they now occupied. The captain himself also rushed to the phone inside the room with him and the leaders as he urgently called for the examiners also. Nevertheless, the examiners reached the room soon after the captain hung up the phone, after requesting their assistance.

Four female doctors and one male nurse entered the room and immediately began to take the alien woman's vital signs. The woman's heart beats stronger than the male nurse has ever heard, as he placed the stethoscope against the woman's chest. Furthermore, one of the female doctors tried to take blood from the woman's hand areas, due to the fact of not being able to locate any veins on the woman's arms. The doctor's needle bent as they tried to pierce the skin of the woman.

The male nurse handed his stethoscope to a different lady doctor in the room so that she can listen to the erratic heartbeat of the woman. The doctor accepted the device and listened as she opened up the eyes of the person inside the pod. The leaders and the captain of the ship asked the medical persons questions and any information regarding her vitals. However, the examiners were Unable to properly answer any questions toward information on the contents of the pod.

Further analysis of the pod would have to be carried out to determine the proper information regarding the care of this operation. Several of the leaders inside the room have been notified to leave the ship and head back to land for a briefing of Mission Monica, from their advisors. The leaders have also been told by the president to leave the pod with the captain of the ship and the medical examiners until a special team could be formed by the president and his secret advisors as well.

The leaders and the captain no longer occupied space with the capsule. The capsule sat alone inside the room with the medical examiners. The president also gave the same instructions to the captain of the ship, as he did the leaders aboard his ship. The woman inside the capsule will receive round the clock medical attention from the president's team of medical supporters. The medical team of the president was trained to notify the president of any changes toward her conditions of health.

Meanwhile, it was clear to see that the woman from another planet was inside of some sort of hibernation and would not awaken. The President of the United States of America's medical team have been dispersed out to sea toward the humanoid woman. Furthermore, all country leaders have started exiting the ship headed for the briefing with the president and his members while the captain sits high in the head of his ship, looking out at land as he watches the emergency flares light up from the beach.

Back inside the room with the pod/capsule, the three lady doctors and the male nurse kept close surveillance on the woman until the president's team will arrive on the ship to take over the mission. However, the woman will remain on the ship until also notified differently from the president. Furthermore, the pod/capsule will leave the ship following the next twenty-four hours for further examination and breakdown.

AWAKENING

Weeks have passed since the world was changed from a crash that took place on one of the most popular beaches in the country of the United States. A woman from another planet sat aboard a ship in a medical coma with no clear date of awakening. The president of America had put together a team of the best medical experts from around the country to overlook the woman from another planet.

Unexpectedly, vital signs increased their speed rapidly, and Sara"s head began to move from each side weakly. Sara"s eyes also have begun to flounder as they tried to break free from their hibernation. Ms. Thomas was assigned as overseer of the project and has stepped away from Sara"s bedside, leaving for the restroom. The nurse inside Sara"s room continued modifying her logs every fifteen minutes, as job instructed. The nurse glanced up from her desk, and out her cubicle toward her very important patient only to notice her struggling to awake.

Sara''s eyes opened very slowly. She immediately began to take in data of her atmosphere. Sara' was not surprised her location was unknown to her. Sara''s large pupils retracted themselves from the bright lights from her heavily guarded room. Sara''s nurse rushed toward her patient, anxious to see what a different life source could offer her own life experience. The nurse was desperate for anything concerning the "awakening" of her patient. Reaching Sara''s bedside, the nurse deeply looked into the eyes of the woman not from her planet.

Sara' looked up into the nurse's eyes and realized that she was some place where she did not belong. She did not seem to understand the creature that stood before her. Sara' focused her sensitive vision on the nurse's face, as she focused reading her facial structure as she continued to motion her head from side to side like a lion staring at its prey with curiosity, just before it kills its dinner.

The nurse appeared in some type of hypnotic trance, as she looked at Sara', mimicking her gestures. Ms. Thomas, now exits the bathroom stall and walks toward the sink to wash her hands. She looked in the mirror and decided to wash her face as well, after appearing to have had a very long day. Meanwhile, the nurse was elevated into the air and Unclothed naked. Sara' Unclothed the nurse after realizing that she herself was nude.

Sara' took control of the nurse, putting her into a hypnotic trance, making the nurse remove her own clothing, for the purpose of clothing herself. The nurse removed her pants first then next her shirt, laying both items on the end of Sara''s bed. The nurse remained in the air, while Sara' tried to sit up in her bed. Sara''s brain was spinning due to her sedation and it took her several attempts to sit up properly. Meanwhile, she allowed the nurse to be let down. She placed both her feet on the floor, balancing the nurse upright.

The nurse walked toward Sara' and placed herself in the bed, taking Sara''s place and positioning herself the same as Sara' had been. Sara' put on the nurse's uniform patiently and headed for the heavily armored iron door. Ms. Thomas had finished rinsing her face off with water and was slightly blinded from the cold water hitting her face. She reached for the paper towels to dry the cold water from her face. Meanwhile, Sara' arrived at the door trying to open it manually. She pushed many bottoms frantically, trying any set of earth numbers that might work.

Sara' backed away from the door, giving herself room to examine the steel door with her black and cloudy white nocturnal eyes. She stared at the hinges of the metal door and they began to come loose noisily. The door melted quickly at its seals and Ms. Thomas has fondly stop wanting to spend time in the restroom and had stopped drying off her face and took one last look at herself in the mirror, before exiting the restroom.

Sara' effortlessly dismantled the door before her, and the nurse struggled to turn her head and pay close attention to Sara' as she was unable to talk or do anything else, to prevent her patient's escape. Sara' finished melting the door at its seals and now pulled the door back without even touching it. The door retrieved backward silently while dripping liquid fragments of itself. Sara' removed the door and placed the door quietly on the floor behind her.

Military guards were at the far end of the hospital hall, and Ms. Thomas exited the restroom headed back toward her patient's room. Ms. Thomas walked down the hall, walking noisily in her government high heel shoes. Sara' popped her head out the opening of her room door and looked to the right of the hallway looking for the guards. The guards were heavily armed and completely dressed in black. They also were equipped with bulletproof black helmets.

Ms. Thomas had ended the hallway and turned right, headed for her prisoner's room. She cut across the hall toward her left and entered the room noticing her client's door lying on her bedroom floor, and immediately looked in the direction of the bed and believed that she sees Sara' lying in her bed. Ms. Thomas turned back toward the door and kneeled down, holding her service revolver looking at the melted door, confused.

Ms. Thomas stood back up and ran to the door, holding her pistol in both her hands. She popped her head out the door and screamed for the guards to come to her aid. The guards were six in total. Ms. Thomas ran to Sara''s bedside only to witness the nurse in some type of paralyzed state. The nurse was unable to speak and hardly capable of moving her head side to side. She was no help in any manner to help in any information leading to Sara''s apprehension.

The nurse had lost control of her bodily functions and had defecated. Thomas covered her mouth from the horrible smell of the nurse's loss of bodily functions, as two of the guards arrived near Ms. Thomas's side. Sara' appeared nowhere in sight as the guard and Ms. Thomas searched the entire stainless steel room for her. However, she appeared missing, forcing the guards to hit the panic bottom alerting the entire facility of a breach in security.

The military ship was entirely occupied by security and armed guards running loosely up and down the hallways of the megaton vessel.

Ms. Thomas screamed, "How could this be that she's not in sight?" She demanded for all security cameras to be scanned. During Ms. Thomas's request of the scanning of the security cameras, doctors rushed into the room. The nurse appeared fully aware. However, her bodily functions were temporally disabled.

Ms. Thomas was notified that video evidence of her prisoner's whereabouts will be available shortly. The video surveillance was uploaded to Ms. Thomas's glasses. The video upload showed Sara' looking around the corner of her door toward the guards before approaching the men. The six guards immediately pulled their weapons at the humanoid. The guards appeared to order Sara' to halt or some order of controlling the situation.

However, Sara' continued to walk toward the guards, disregarding their apparent orders. She continued to walk forward as they yelled for her to stop. Sara' was slightly larger than the guards. She approached closer within firing distance of the military guards. The guards backed up, allowing Sara' extra time to reason with herself. Sara' sped up and the guards had no choice but to put the woman down.

Shots were fired at the woman not from earth. Twenty-four bullets were fired toward Sara'. She stopped the bullets from hitting her by a force not known to men. The bullets stopped suspended in air as she continued closer toward the guards. The men pulled out metal electric rods in self-defense. The men were frozen by Sara' and made to put away their service weapons and electric sticks.

Sara' continued completely past the bullets, only to have the bullets follow behind her slowly like angry police dogs. The guards were now finished putting away their weapons and stood in military formation against the walls of the hallway. Sara' had taken control of the guards, and had taken their memories of her and the incident, giving the guards temporary amnesia.

Sara' moved past the guards and turned left down the hallways, with the bullets following behind her. The guards resumed their laughter and silent joking. Suddenly one of the men spotted Ms. Thomas coming and alerted the rest of his team and all the men stood in formation until Ms. Thomas entered the room out of their sight. The camera located inside Sara''s room also showed Sara' undressing the nurse and taking the nurse's clothing for her own.

Ms. Thomas shut the image off her glasses and headed down the hallway with more than twenty armed men and women following closely behind her in search of Sara'. The nurse had gained control of her bodily functions and gasped for air as she screams for her mother. However, Sara' headed further down the hallway, appearing to connect with her senses of north, east, west, and south.

Sara' continued further down the hall, approaching rooms with other patients apparently, but not like her or the creatures of this earth. Turning left, Sara' marched forward heading west, toward the end of a hallway. She glanced to the left and noticed a doctor from this planet dissecting a live humanoid creature, which was screaming for its life. Sara' looked through the glass motionlessly, saddened for the screaming alien and allows the bullets that followed her to slowly bump up against the bulletproof glass. The bullets continued to bump up against the glass until they all barricaded themselves into the thick glass headed for the male doctor dissecting the live alien creature.

The doctor was disturbed from cracking sounds that broke through the creature's screams. The doctor turned toward the sound of glass cracking and was surprised to find a tall, beautiful woman standing behind his cracking operating room window. The doctor slowly walked up to the glass while pulling away his face mask from his face. The doctor could not fully appreciate this women's beauty, as his mouth remained ajar as he now stood before the window. However, the bullet's continued to move through the protective glass until they made contact with the male doctor from earth.

The doctor stood there until he was hit by the bullets and killed. It was as if he wanted to die just so he could have a good look at Sara' Leon. The protective glass that sat between Sara' and the alien creature looked like Swiss cheese from the bullets that passed through it. There were three nylon ropes that secured the screaming creature to the bed. Sara' released the creature by unfastening the ropes from around the alien's body. The creature jumped from its bed quickly and begun to run only to have its intestines hit the floor and pouring from its belly. The doctor unfortunately did not die without taking the creature's life with his.

Meanwhile, Ms. Thomas and other military personnel searched through the large ship for the large alien woman. The president also had been made aware of Sara''s possible escape from the ship out at sea. Nevertheless, Sara' had seen enough and left the area of the dead doctor and alien being. Continuing to walk amongst the ship's many tunnels and hallways, Sara' searched for the exit that led to the deck of the military ship.

Sara' walked through the military vessel as if she had designed the craft herself, as she appeared to know which way to exactly maneuver. Sara' continued to make a minimum of turns before she would reach her destination which was the chest of the ship—in other words, the deck of the ship. Reaching the deck of the ship, Sara' was met by Ms. Thomas and her many dangerous members. The deck of the ship was occupied by hundreds of men and women who helped operate the military vessel.

Sara' had hundreds of eyes on her on the chest of the ship. Ms. Thomas was handed a blow horn and spoke through the devise.

"Please give up peacefully and lie on the deck of the ship. We come in peace. I promise, we mean you no harm, can you understand me?"

Many military men and women now had their weapons pointed at the alien woman. oddly, a voice came over the intercom of the ship. The voice was not recognized from anyone aboard the military vessel.

"I will rule this planet and I wish to speak to the one or the individuals who run this world!"

Ms. Thomas and hundreds of others looked for the source of the voice, only to come up empty with suggestions later. Sara''s mouth never opened but it did not take long before the woman from Adamen was connected to the source of the strange voice.

Sara' turned from her followers and toward land, and walked overboard falling into the deep ocean water. Hundreds of crewmembers rushed toward the side of their ship to look for the woman overboard. The president was further informed of Sara''s escape and suicidal attempt. He hang up the phone and rubbed his bald head. The president's phone lit up with many different colors as each color stood for a different country. The allied countries of America wanted to be updated of the alien woman's whereabouts.

BATTLE FOR AMERICA

Swimming under the Atlantic Ocean in an attempt to escape being captured by the ship *Earl*, Sara' searched for the leader of America. Meanwhile, military personnel as well as police departments around the world increased their security presence throughout the country searching for Sara' Leon. The nocturnal woman was able to evade the government hiding under the subzero temperatures of the Atlantic Ocean. Sara' walked onto the soil of New York City. In a short amount of time, she walked through Times Square searching for the president of the United States of America.

Standing on the sidewalk of Times Square, she looked at a television monitor located high in the sky above one of the city's high-rises. A picture of the president came on the local news issuing a warning to the American citizens: Hello, people of America, a day has come when we must come together as an nation. There was a crash off the coast of Santa Monica, California, and upon the crash, there was a being inside, much similar to one of use; however, the being inside was a woman from another planet, approximately six feet in height and very pale-skinned. The woman also is a nocturnal being with large, slanted eyes, making her capable of a night life. If you see this individual, don't hesitate to pick up your phones and contact authorities.

Pedestrians, walking past Sara' watching the president deliver his address recognized her from the picture on the large screen monitor and ran in fear for their lives.

After watching the news broadcast, Sara' vanished from the pedestrians' vision, disappearing and reappearing in front of the lawn of the White House. People on the streets who witnessed Sara' standing on the streets of New York called the police department and military armed forces in their district. However, Sara' now stood in front of the White House in search of the free people's leader. Sara' walked toward the white house gates and immediately jumped the fence, and walked through the grass only to be detected from several motion sensors made to detect unlawful entry.

The sensors were heat and motion activated, and Sara''s movement caused alarms to ring out and send guards rushing toward her as she walked through the grass. Guards of the White House carried electric nets ready for their attack on her. However, Sara' flung her left hand forward toward the approaching guards with their nets, and their bodies began to be pulled apart; the guards' skeletons started to remove itself from their flesh.

The blood from the guards' bodies remained airborne once the bones were removed, leaving their bodies pale from the loss of blood. Several more guards rushed forward, as if what just happened was not visible to them.

Additional alarms were set off from the commotion and the White House glowed florescent orange. Dozens of guards appeared from many areas surrounding the White House's lawn in search for Sara'. The guards surrounded the humanoid woman quickly and opened fire on Sara', giving the murderous harlot, all she could handle, considering she wished to kill all who existed for the purpose of controlling the male population. The armed guards believed that they were giving the future queen all she could handle, by releasing tens of dozens of rounds of deadly weapon fire. The guards believed.

The bullets from the guards' guns exploded as each guard pulled their trigger from their service weapons. Many of the guards' hands and fingers were destroyed from the explosive gunpowder which blew many of their fingers off. Many men lay on the ground wounded and screaming as Sara' approached them. There were a total of twenty-six men screaming for help lying in the grass of the White House. Sara' held out both of her arms forward, as if she wished the guards to rise standing on their feet.

The men stood at attention facing the humanoid woman with fear and tears in their eyes, and their chest cavities were heavy with freight. All the men were parlayed standing in the lawn of the White House, standing motionless as Sara' stood before them calmly. The servicemen appeared confused, as if something Unfamiliar had taken control over their bodies, because the men were only capable of moving their heads. Blood suddenly began to be pulled from every direction from the guard's weakened bodies, until all of their blood was removed and reformed into the shape of very large circular beach ball.

Sara' placed her right arm besides her right leg, with her fingers pointed toward the ground and her left hand toward the gate which she had moments ago jumped across. Six of the guards were herald toward the fence. The guards hit the gate, slicing their bodies. Pedestrians stood on the streets of Washington, witnessing murder and devastation unfold in front of their very eyes.

The president watched his men's dismantlement from television monitors located inside the White House. Tears journeyed down the face of America's leader, the president mumbled, "So help us God."

Sara' placed down her left arm by her side, and motioned the beach ball-sized blood into the White House, causing the president's home to appear satanically sacrificed.

The remaining nineteen guard's bodies were dispersed throughout the White House structure, causing holes to be shot throughout the building of the White House. Body parts flew through the White House, making the First Lady to clutch her children tightly against her bosom, crying for their safety. Television cameras and world news have arrived on the street outside the White House. Sara' approached the heavily secured doors, and without speaking, demanded the door to destroy itself, causing smoke to appear before her!

Military personnel and the Secrete Service entered the city's emergency address, to aid the presidential protection order. Meanwhile, the president and his family were gathered up by his body guards. "Come, Mr. President, we must evacuate you and your family now!" a guard told the president. The first family was brought to an emergency elevator that led the protective family several levels below the city streets of Washington, DC. Sara' walked through the White House, only to be met by more gunfire.

Panicked service officers' fired shots, rung the air penetrating the Secret Service men's eardrums. Sara' was so addictively attractive that the guards stopped shooting and stared with amazement at this woman. Sara' walked closer toward the guards and hypnotized them, making the men lead her to the direction of the first family of the United States of America.

Sara' now stood before the president and looks deeply inside of his soul, and sees a small boy child crying on his bed alone, while his mother entertained many different men over the young president's home. The young president was his mother's only child and being alone was not easy to deal with. The young president's mother wanted desperately to replace his father because her lifestyle required much attention as well and she sought attention from numerous strange men.

However, Mrs. President held her, and her husband's children firmly against her breast. The servicemen who led Sara' to the president were made to stand in the same room as the first family and Sara'. Mrs. President was asked to quite down from her husband. Sara' turned toward the servicemen, and they all began to scream with pain. The men's eyes began to bleed from their slants, and so did their ears. Suddenly one of the servicemen's arms broke backward, and the children of the first family screamed loudly.

The president screamed and instantly a different serviceman neck twisted backward and his face turned purple from suffocation and loss of blood. Sara' gestured to the First Lady to walk next to her husband with her two small children, one of whom was a boy and the other a young girl.

Also, the president himself was motioned to take a seat at his desk. Now the first family was together and unit in one location sitting and standing behind the president's desk, centered in the rear of his large room. Three of the guards remained, from the six initial service men. Three men remained standing just feet from the entrance of the protective room below Washington's public streets. The men each had their weapons pointed at the door ready to fire their guns at anything entering the room with Sara' and the first family.

The president asked the tall un-earthly women, "What it that you wish of me, and of my planet?" However, Sara' responded no immediate words at first. Sara' continued to look at the president until he climbed on top of his desk, lying on his back with both his arms beside his body. Sara' walked toward the president and lifted up his neck with her hands, cuffing the back of his head talking to his mind. Is this your planet? No, it isn't. Then I wish to speak with who employs you? The president allowed tears to continue to flow down his face before his mind was made to release an image to the woman murderer visually.

Abruptly, the First Lady asked Sara': please don't kill me or my children. Sara' looked in the direction of the First Lady and instantly the First Lady's eyes turned completely white as milk. Sara' had taken away the First Lady's vision, blinding her to silence her suffering. Meanwhile, Sara' looked back down into the president's eyes and continued to speak with him.

The president of America: I will agree to introduce you to my higher ups in command. Sara' had allowed the leader to stand up and be with his family. The president ran toward his wife and grabbed her, trying to keep her calm and quiet from making any further noise as he took into consideration that his wife's vision had been taken away from her. The First Lady screamed with panicked fear, from her loss of sight. "Honey, it's going to be okay," the president told his wife.

The children never cried with fear because Sara' had placed a vision of joyfulness into the young children's minds. They walked away from their father and crying mother, and went to sit down and play in a corner of the large underground office. Sara' focused her view importantly on the president as she backed up toward the door of his office. Sara' faced the door and did not look back toward the president. Instead, she walks entirely out the room and back in the direction which she had come from.

The retrieval from the president's office was rather quiet and offered no threat of danger to Sara' or her recruits, the servicemen of the White House. Blood covered the walls and so did many bullet holes from the previous battle earlier. Also noticing, emergency fire sprinklers and soft red emergency lights bounced off the white paint of the walls.

Sara' appeared to have tunnel vision as she was escorted levels up on Washington public streets from her secret service men, made available from the president's security team. The emergency elevator now was in view and had been entered by Sara'. Two of the servicemen halted outside the elevator and one entered the contraption allowing the nocturnal woman full escort and protection. Sara' stood in the elevator looking out, and the other two servicemen entered after Sara' to secure and protect the future Queen of earth.

No words have been spoken between the service men or Sara'. All communication remained nonverbal. The elevator doors completely shut close and one of the servicemen selected a code that would lead the elevator upstairs and into the White House lobby. The elevator rose and its motion was detected as it traveled up different level and floors.

SWAT team officials sat outside the White House and studied many blueprints mapping the White House's floor plans, for the purpose of locating the First Family. The correct floor plan was chosen and the president was located three stories below the city streets. The First Family was located from monitors inside the president's office, and the president and his family appeared frantically shaken and in need of medical attention.

The highly sensitive camera system of the White House had also spotted Sara' and her protectors. The group had entered the main lobby of the White House and the lobby door was in view of the street. Sara' and the servicemen walked out the lobby and into the lawn heading toward the streets. SWAT had sniper view of Sara' and the men who escorted the alien woman outside.

Sara' was told over loudspeaker from a swat negotiator: stop and place yourself on the ground. The servicemen who walked along with Sara', were ordered as well. Police and television cameras also zeroed in on the nocturnal woman, while they hid behind public service vehicles. Sara' and the men never stopped moving forward. SWAT ordered Sara' and the servicemen to stop again, yet they still refused to follow their orders.

SWAT, was given the command to take lethal shots at the group. Sniper fire was released, and one of the three servicemen walking with Sara' was struck in the head and killed. One of the two remaining servicemen picked up his dead teammate's weapon and abruptly opened fire on SWAT and officers guarding the public streets of Washington, DC.

Sara' took over the men's vision and made the men become perfect murderous weapons. The men moved swiftly and released many shots at the outside crowds of people, killing many innocent pedestrians and government officials. The remaining two servicemen moved at speeds that were supernatural, speeds over forty miles an hour.

SWAT and other protective agencies opened fire enthusiastically on Sara' and her two followers. The servicemen hide themselves behind trees firing back at SWAT members and police officers. Several more SWAT and officers were hit from Sara"s two protectors. Sara"s men had perfect deadly accurate kill shots, hitting many of the officers and SWAT in the heads with bullets that penetrated their helmets easily.

Officer's bullets struck the trees that sheltered the two men hiding behind them. Sara' herself engaged in open gunfire also. She placed both of her arms forward and stopped the bullets from hitting her. She made the bullets melt before they could be capable of hitting her body. The bullets appeared to have struck an invisible shield, a shield which protected Sara'.

Sara' faced a group of officers wounded from gunfire hiding behind a severely bullet-riddled police vehicle. The group was spotted because one of the wounded officers in the group relentlessly continued to return fire, placing herself and her group in jeopardy of being purposely targeted. The riddled police vehicle noticeably started to move and the officers hiding behind the vehicle looked up from their sitting down position, wondering what made the car move.

The officers tried desperately escaping the moving police car as quickly as their wounded bodies would allow, but the car quickly folded itself in half, smashing and killing the hidden and wounded officers. Very little of the remaining officers and SWAT enforcement personnel have noticed their other members smashed and killed from the folded police vehicle. The fight with the woman from Adamen caused many humans to lose track of what was important.

Oddly, gunfire stopped and Sara"s hidden servicemen came from behind the trees to stand in open view of the officers' kill shots. One men placed his weapons in his holster while the other threw the extra weapon away from their dead partner. The servicemen walked on opposite sides of Sara'.

Sara' continued forward and the servicemen followed closely behind her. Sara' looked around the entire sector of police who barricaded the streets outside the main entrance of the White House. Sara also looked up at the rooftops and windows at the SWAT team snipers. Sara' walked and in her same motion, she winked very slowly and the officers pulled out their weapons from their holsters and opened fire on each other. Snipers began to shot the officers below on the streets, taking only head shots, killing the officers instantly.

Sara' and her service officers walked calmly through the gunfire viewing the destruction and the officers killing themselves. The scene was bloody. It was inhumanly possible to keep one's nerves by watching the lives being taken. Vastly the ground shooting was quiet, everyone in the department of public defense was dead and killed. Some of the bodies lying on the ground shook from their nerves twitching.

Unsuspectingly, half a dozen shots disturbed the silence of the atmosphere once again. The snipers have begun to kill each other, as Sara' glanced up at the windows and rooftops. Television camera people ran away in the opposite direction of Sara', as she walked in their direction. The television people were not harmed by Sara' or the bullets of the officers killing each other.

Automobiles burned on the streets of Washington, DC, from bullets hitting their gas tanks and people throwing bottle bombs at the vehicles attempting to strike Sara', as they tried to help the police and other members of government. Sara' headed west of Pennsylvania toward New York avenue. Sara' crossed the street when she noticed a chubby news reporter woman hiding on the side of a burning building. Sara' made her lips move, releasing the words, "Come here, earth woman."

The chubby reporter held her camera proudly up on her shoulders, unsure of how to properly operate the equipment, she did what Sara' asked of her. Sara' and the servicemen stopped abruptly in the reporter's path. The reporter focused her camera into the face of Sara'. Sara' stared with a purpose into the television camera and said, "Threat from within this country, comes many lives lost. I will be the river of life for this planet!"

CONCENTRATION CAMPS!

America was defeated. The new queen wasted no time in controlling America, and making the men of the country register for pickup. Also including all male children from eleven and a half years of age must register for the camps as well. No male gender should remain free on the streets Unsupervised, or without proper registration forms. Many months have passed since the country was taken over and many women were given positions as overseers of the men of America. Many of Sara"s workers were volunteers who understood the meaning of a better society. Registration was surgically implanted inside of every male testicle sac, and once the implant was connected, the adult male, or young male; would become immediately connected with the Male National Security Unit, or MNSU. Meanwhile, other countries around the globe are scrambling to put up some type of offence toward this cancer that will soon engulf the entire plant.

However, Mothers from around the country of America continued to cry from losing their babies/boys. The young boys would cry and beg for their mothers' help before they were medically put to sleep before their operations. Some young boys grabbed and pulled on their mother's hair and cleavage before leaving with doctors and security personnel. Sara' positioned women to lead the world, and only the top elite women will participate in any form of decision making. The gates for registration were located in key sections around the country, in such places as California, Colorado, Texas, New Jersey, Tennessee, and lastly, the state of Maine.

Millions of people voluntarily entered the camps, at the request of Sara', and their government; however, many people living in the camps, were sick and died prematurely. People in the camps died due to stomach viruses and heart infections to which heart worms would root itself to the human heart and next destroy the human lungs. Furthermore, some type of unknown breakout inside the camps began to kill large numbers of males. Many people died in the camps, before any word was made public.

Young boys who reached the age of twelve now resided in the camps and were made to take showers amongst hundreds of older men during any particular part of the day, considering what time the outside showers would pop up from under the ground. The showers would pop up in numerous locations around the camps. The showers were thick poles that rose from beneath the ground. The poles were eight feet in height, and designed to shoot water more than twenty feet into the air, and when gravity pulled the water back toward the ground, each person would become entirely invisible to the next individual showering besides them.

The camps were open terrain that ran for hundreds of miles in any direction. It would take hours to feed the large majority of the camp population, and some people living in the camps would not eat for days at a time, consequently from the length of the long chow lines. The chow lines were twenty lines wide in width, and one line could stretch over five miles long, any day of the week.

The chow lines resembled the New York subway stations from the year 2015. Men would walk toward the bars of the chow entrances, and the bars would scan the men for feeding, according to their electric chips readings located inside their testicles. Many young children died from malnutrition and heart disease inside the camps, and older men would show the young boys no love. Instead, the older males continued to pass over the young boys' weakened bodies lying on the ground. Furthermore, some young boys were killed and raped for entertainment purposes. The young boys would scream and cry for help, only to have no one interested in helping them.

The camps were brutal toward the juveniles, and many of the young children did not survive long. The adult males would huddle together, trying to reserve any type of nutrition possible. However, many of the young boys would wonder around the campgrounds whimpering for their mothers and fathers. Any father who had children inside the camps were relocated to different facilities in order to keep out resistance toward the guards guarding the camps. Some fathers who had children inside the camps would fight the guards for their children's safety, and others would not. They would instead push their young sons along with the armed guards. Some fathers hugged their children for the last times whispering in their sons' ears, "Go with the guards."

The kids were hurried along making the emotional moments of their departure from their fathers move along swiftly. The guards were trained to examine behavior and body motion, in order to defuse and deescalate situations. Numerous fathers and different son groups were loaded onto trucks and driven away to different camp locations, and relocated to different cities and towns around America. The camps were surrounded by barbwire and high towers with armed women guards with high-powered rifles. The women guards were trained to take head shots only. The prisoners of the camps understood the rules of their living conditions, and one of the most important rule of the camps was that, under no circumstance, should any resident of the camp walk in any group of more than two at any given time. Registration was inevitable for many American citizens, who versioned the registration chip being introduced to the world during their time living on God's green earth, as a sign of the mark of the beast. The chip was implanted long before the public was decided to have a say so in the matter, of their well-being.

Registration chips, also known as the RC/implant, was unknowingly passed out from key locations around the country. The chip was first passed out at local drug stores, in the disguise of a local flu shot. The surgical chip made it impossible to escape the net of Sara"s control. There were many people who would rather die than to become subjected to having being forced to live with the registration chip; those individual were driven off and away from the camps inside of red and yellow crew vans, and never seen again or they died of sudden illnesses.

Sara' launched order and control over the people of America, and forces numbers of aggression upon the people of the free land. The American male was felt to be a creature of Uncertainty and an individual of no spiritual belief, or lack of discipline. Sara' allowed her instincts to take control of her, and decided to filter out the United States of America. There was no escape from the camps or from registration. Her plan was very well organized and many fleeing people will be captured.

Thousands of people, thought that they would not be able to just merely turn themselves in to the proper authorities, and walk away from residence from Sara''s concentration camps. Thousands of males whom fled from future residence from the camps were arrested at grocery stores and even simple places such as local car washes. People around the country of America were surgically implanted with Sara''s chip and it made the people of the country easy to apprehend individually or in large numbers.

Children's elementary schools, junior, and high schools were empty of occupants due to the fear of registration. There have been many terrifying tales of the camps and the people who lost their lives behind the queen's gates. Sara' immediately took hardship on the United States of America. It was as if Sara' had an intuition of the country and the males who lead their country in leadership.

Registration was decided long ago when the queen was a teenager on her planet. Sara' was innocent when her mother and younger sister were killed by dangerous men who wished to kill her father. Sara' shortly after witnessed her mother and sister being killed and narrowly escaped with her own life, found out some time later that her father laid in the back ground hiding, as he also witnessed his wife and younger daughter murdered. The killers made young Sara' lie on the ground and face toward her mother and younger sister, while one of the killers poured high doses of deadly mineral acid on her mother and sister.

The type of minerals that was poured on Sara"s mother and sister was a flesh and fiber eating acid. Sara"s mother and sister screamed shortly with a great amount of pain and agony in their voices. The mineral acid ate holes in their faces and head quickly, killing any noise of life that could have remained. Young Sara' laid on the ground with a large male from her planet stepping on her neck; however, Sara' did not make any sound, she laid on the ground and faced her dying mother and sister, while she blinked her eyes continuously, crying silently.

The killers of Sara"s mother and sister allowed Sara' up from the floor of her home so she could try and revive her loved ones. Sara' crawled to her mother and sister quickly, but she dared not touch them, Sara' just sat there in front of them and hung her head low, Sara' was very angry and full of rage, but the young queen could not allow herself to do anything because the males were more powerful than Sara'.

There were three large male standing behind Sara' as she mourned for her sister and mother. The males only stayed shortly after killing her sister and mother. The males all turned around at different times, before exiting Sara"s parents' home, Sara' walked down a hallway of her home, to her sleeping quarters and retrieved a large sheet and placed it over her deceased mother and sister. Sara' never checked the door after the large males exited her home. Instead she shut off all the lights in her home with her powers and looked out a window of her home.

Sara' looked out the window and spotted her father hiding behind several trees near the forest behind her home. Sara' sensed her father and his fear for his own life, as he hid from the killers who murdered his family. Sara''s father looked toward the dark window of his home and spoke the words to his daughter telepathically, how he loved her and he was truly sorry for her sister and mother. Sara' cried even harder during that moment. Sara' cried loudly as she watched her father run to the rear of the forest behind her home, fleeing with embarrassment and sorrow from losing his family.

The young queen of earth vowed to never let any male hurt her or dominate her in any type of form again. This memory was just one of few occurrences that sparked the reason for registration of all males. Sara' believed that she must rule and govern her own world and make her planet predictable for safety. No male will walk the streets until the queen found it fit for the male population, to once again walk the streets, of the free world of America!

REGISTRATION!

“Greetings, world, and all my joining nations. I made a previous decision about the male population of Earth, beginning in America. However, not all of you have committed yourselves to my order; therefore, there will be vehicles inside of every neighborhood and community to pick up all illegal males. The males will be relocated to areas Unknown, until notified differently from your queen! Any males caught after pickup date will be detained and executed! All males immediately upon the age of thirteen years of age must be fully registered for pickup and transfer.”

The camps where full of depressed and antisocial children. Families from across the world watched Sara”s concentration camp speech. Husbands and wives cried and hugged their children close, fearing for their family’s safety. Some families immediately started to pack their most valuable belongings for the sake of fleeing and hiding, trying to evade capture. People looked out of their home windows and doors paranoid, of the time of pickup.

Small children were crying, because they couldn't perceive why their mothers and fathers were running through their home upset, and knocking over things in their houses! People were now running down the streets screaming and running in many directions. However, Earth's new queen continued to speak across America's televisions networks. "People of planet Earth, escape is not possible, I have arrived to adopt your home as my own."

The United States military was under full authority of Sara' and stood by waiting for further instruction. The president was viewed standing behind Sara' as she publicly delivered her instructions of all camp pickups. Sara' spoke, "People, it is December 28, 2028, and within forty-eight hours military vehicles will begin entry into neighborhoods around the country."

Television cameras shut off around America, after Sara' finished addressing the country, giving the people contemplating time about the news that have shocked so many worldwide. The First Lady stood beside her husband, crying of the new world order that was taking place. However, Sara' faced forward inside the briefing room located in the middle of the White House focused on the noise of the First Lady.

Sara' turned around fully and faced the First Lady, motioning her head from different angles as if she was trying to understand her reasons for crying. The First Lady stopped crying and tightened up her dress collar, trying to quit herself, fearful of Sara''s uncertainties. Sara''s height allowed her to slightly look over the president's head. However, she towered over his wife and intimidated her sobbing her silent.

Sara' finished looking over the first family, observing them carefully before she walked out the room, leaving the negative threat of Adolf Hitler's concentration camps of the nineteenth century, embedded into the American people's mind countrywide. After the presidential weekly briefing, millions of Americans searched for any firearm they might have in their homes, or any place or person on the street that could sell them one, that would allow any resistance toward being forced to reside in the camps.

Shockingly, many Americans owned high caliber weapons and ammunition despite of a passed bill to remove all high caliber weapons out the hands of many of their countrymen and women's homes. Neighbors ran to neighbor's houses seeking help and support toward the new beginning for their shaky country. Some citizens of the country have underground bunkers, well aware of a time such as this one when many did not.

The concentration camps were already in construction and housed millions already around different parts of the country; however, there are many illegal men running free around the country who believe that registration can be avoided. The American people were fully unaware of the camps existence or progress. Members of the American government were quieting any whispers of the camps due to the day of a time such as this. The government wanted to use the campgrounds against the people of their country to filter their own people out. Sara' was given secret reports of this country's future world order, from people who secretly was in charge, a society of men who have passed down power from one generation of people to the next and selected family members.

Sara' decided to utilize America's plans against their own people, and initiate the illegal pick-up early. Many American people tried evacuating major populated cities and highways around their country. Traffic became congested for miles along the roads and highways. Small children cried in the back seats of their parent's vehicle, as they looked out their parent's car windows to monitor other children's tears of wariness also.

People flooded and violated public transportation laws, and proceed to drive their electric cars and bikes over traffic height restrictions. Many vehicles attempted to flee and escape in numerous directions, families drove their bikes and cars over trees and zigzag across neighboring highways high in the air. The fleeing motorist were quickly apprehended and chased down from helicopters with highly dangerous weapon fire. The people were warned by the military aircrafts to join the other pedestrians back on to public highways, or deadly force could be an issue of concern.

Several vehicles were shot down out the air and crashed into trees and large land fields in the area. And other motor crafts were electronically directed back to their homes and apartment buildings. The vehicles were controlled around the country, from military control panels secretly hidden from the public inside the vehicle's brain. Sara' notified the people of this land that escape would be impossible.

All major roads were blocked off by government personnel preventing any further confusion of the fleeing people's attempted escapes. Many began to exit their motor vehicles and stormed the protective barricades of military and law enforcement. Military people pulled their weapons and pointed them at the innocent people approaching their barricades.

Government personnel monitored the commotion from their office buildings and from home. A decision was reached from the American government to send all cars and motor bikes home for the purpose of clearing the roads, making the streets accessible for further concerns. All vehicles occupying the streets were considered smart cars and can be controlled from their manufactures or the government.

The government made the decision to put in place Operation Factory Reset to avoid any further death on their own people, contradictory to their future plans of filtering their people. Suddenly, many of the vehicles rose from the streets and headed toward their primary addresses, clearing the city streets and roads. A large majority of people were outside their vehicles fueling further panic and chaos by screaming at the officials guarding the barricades, when unsuspectingly their cars, trucks, and bikes began to head home without their occupants.

Thousands of people looked up into the sky, wondering how their vehicles must operate themselves. Others remained in their vehicles trapped and unable to operate the vehicles or free themselves. Looking up, the sky was filled with what appeared to be millions of motor crafts and screaming people who were panicked of the elevation of the cars and trucks, driving through the sky manually by themselves.

However, other places around the country people looted grocery stores taking anything at their disposal. Many of the more intelligent looters went after bottled water and batteries. Other people raided gas stations for their nuclear battery cells that gave power to their vehicles. Many fires burned around the cities of America, making the sky black in numerous locations in the country's sky. People began to aggressively assault each other and steal things that others had stolen for their own survival.

The time was 3:00 p.m. and it had only been five hours since Sara' notified the American population of her decision of the illegal male population entering the camps. News and government helicopters patrolled the air, recording all chaos and events of the attempted escapes of their fellow countrymen. However, all helicopters flying the sky received hostile gunfire from angered pedestrians.

Sara' could not allow any illegal male to roam America's streets, and decided to move the pickup date early for the unresided. Meanwhile, a small majority of people never left their homes for food or fuel for their vehicles. Instead, they hid in their homes, boarding up all and any windows. Many pedestrians still roamed the streets outside their neighborhoods appearing to be misplaced.

The sun now wished to set itself in this part of the world. The people of America all seemed to understand that time was not on their side because after all, who knows what the morning would bring the people. The sky darkened quickly from the help of many burning buildings and vehicles throughout the countryside. Satellite photos showed images of hot spots around the country from terrified people destroying their country.

Neighboring countries viewed America's hopelessness from the temporary safety of their country's borders. The country of America was granted no help from her allies. No one wanted to voluntarily involve themselves in the death wish that was taking place in the great country.

American people have never contemplated such things were possible for the people. Instead, they believed they were excluded from attacks such as this. Sara"s arrival showed the country that history repeats old behaviors. People drank coffee and conversed into the late and early hours of the morning, trying to be the first ones to spot the trucks entering into their communities.

A neighborhood located inside of south central California was the first to be visited by gigantic trucks with the letters PC, which stood for Population Control, and others had the letters FEMA. The city was known for its race riot of the year 1992. The riot was named the Rodney King riots. The streets that occupied the large trucks were Florence and Normandy. A small child looked out the windows of his mother's apartment, and spotted the gigantic trucks in the early morning hours.

Martial law began for American citizens. No sixth amendment rights, and the executive branch to implement military oversight over civilian affairs, the government legislation will allow for the retention and torture of American citizens as combatants, all for the greater good of the American people. National Guard officials arrived in the neighborhood before all other military personnel.

The National Guard had practiced for a moment such as this one, and the name of the training was called disaster training. Second group government personnel was the local police department. The officers visited the neighborhood of south central on horseback armed with pepper guns and semi-automatic weapons capable of releasing live bursts of nonlethal rounds of rubber bullets, and others carried weapons of deadly force, that would be used as last effort attempts of controlling disagreeing societies.

Helicopters and airplanes aided invading enforcement agencies by flying over the land of south central and scanning the houses and ground for irregular temperatures from people hiding underground, attempting to escape the threats of urban warfare. Police and National Guard members alike notified the people of Los Angeles to remain indoors until personnel retrieves each household one at a time. The notification alerted many residents of the pickup.

People disobeyed the orders and come outside their homes attempting to ask questions, only to be met by the loudspeakers commanding them to go back inside their homes or force would be used. Hundreds and quickly to be thousands, of armed military people and police officers now dominated American streets rounding up the illegal people of the free country.

War began for the country of America. How terrifying the threat came from within the country. Many people fired shots out the windows of apartment buildings and from behind commercial buildings. It would seem the people of Los Angeles would fight back in order to protect their freedom. Many people in this city had firearms. Many gang members opened fire on any person wearing a uniform of any sort.

Bullets penetrated many homes and killed innocent people. Helicopters threw nets from above onto people running in the streets and those people where soon apprehended and placed inside the trucks. Many people were killed openly in the streets, and that reaction caused hundreds of citizens to turn themselves in for transfer and release to the camps.

The battle went on for quite some time, late in the month of December before the people understood that their battle against the government would be short lived, for many fighting to resist their oppressors. The takeover of Los Angeles, California, was viewed worldwide, adding to Sara"s dominant reputation. South central could not win their urban war with the American government and was made an example of the raft to further apprehend the United States.

Many people around the United States became political prisoners of the camps. Hundreds of people also occupied empty spaces in city streets as they lay wounded and dying from blunt force trauma from brutal forces of control from their government, whom aided the Queen. Quickly as the people from Los Angeles were captured, they were delivered to Sara"s camps. After California initiated the order of illegal pick, many states around the country, was given the message to begin capture and pickup, of the remaining illegal males, in their section of the region.

Inside the camps, the dead quickly outnumbered the living. The weak and dying slept with the dead inside the camps. However, the weak was buried amongst the dead, space was needed for the illegals. People who were buried with the dead cried from below in their graves, as dirt was poured on their still breathing bodies. Massive graves were dug. The graves were nine feet wide and more than thirty feet long in their length.

Dozens of the dead died from open and infected wounds and others had deadly cases of tuberculosis from being closely confined with other camp prisoners. People around the camps began to speak to themselves and have full conversations with invisible beings. The people's minds have been broken due to severe beatings, and hundreds of killings per day have taken a toll on many innocent people and caused their minds to break.

The stench around the camps was Unbearable. The camps were execution camps and more than three hundred died every day inside the camps. The dead were cremated five hundred bodies every twelve hours. The dead had numbers and their nationalities written on their stomachs, so that their bodies could be recorded for the exact number of casualties.

The state of California soon appeared abandoned of all males who once resided in the state. Women owned all jobs and will soon run their states. Buses and schools alike were empty of male life, and the male population will soon become extinct, it would seem. Sara' managed to keep track of all life in the state of California, and soon Sara' will be able to monitor the world.

People who tried to remain hidden under public streets were apprehended long ago, which made the terra surreal to see any male on public streets. However, some males were allowed to remain free on the streets with the proper registration papers. Also males whom owned the proper papers, had jobs such as police officers, fire fighters, special tactic teams of protection, and so on.

Seven months after Sara' had taken over American, and had managed to capture all males, Order had naturally began to take its course and life around America started to move forward productively once again. The Queen ordered a team of her soldiers and neighboring countries to enter and cease control of the African continent, and stop the angry and violent country, from killing each other and also to send home all of the country's interferences.

Life inside the camps was harsh and millions of people lost their lives inside these death camps. However, human life could sustain and evolve through some of the most extreme and toughest conditions. People tried to fight and resist their queen's order of control, but the inevitable took place. Sara' wished for predictability, so she sent a team to the country of Africa to oversee order and control over the reckless and dangerous country.

Sara' needed no help in ceasing Africa; however, the queen wanted to observe her joining forces strength. Africa appeared easy to apprehend for the nations and would be perfect practice for moments ahead of Earth.

TAKEOVER OF AFRICA!

United Nations and American soldiers we're over taken from the united African nations. The entire country of Africa fought as an angry mother lion, fighting for the life of her cubs against the queen's armies. Millions of bullets pierced the air killing members of both sides fighting, the American and United Nations. The Africans fought guerilla warfare, the people of the African country used weapons such as machetes, hand grenades, and nearly all residents owned semi- or full automatic weapons.

Rocket launchers were used by the African people to destroy heavy machinery, used by the United Nations. The natives of Africa were using animals of their wild land as guard animals. Many people of Africa, commonly young men, owned hyenas as their animal of choice. The Americans and their joining nations had only the common domestic dog, and the dogs of choices were the cane corco, the Argentinean mastiff, the Boerboel, and fondly the German Shepherd.

The Africans released their hyenas as they opened fire, killing the armed soldiers of the earth's new queen, while simultaneously allowing their killer pets to attack the domestic dogs of the soldiers from overseas. However, these particular breeds were killers by rights of their titles. The dogs held their own for some time until they were tired, and once the domestic dogs tired, the hyenas began to bite the dogs while removing chunks of flesh, causing the dogs to suffer before bleeding to death and dying.

Worldwide, the country of Africa was known as the "Blinder." Many different countries have volunteered to participate in some type of aid for the country of Africa in some sort of way. The atmosphere inside the country could be intimidating for a person not of the native blood, reported from volunteers from many different countries who passed aid in the country in support. The people of Africa instinctively understood war, and it flowed through the blood in their veins. However, many of the people fled to fields and hid themselves among the long grass because of the fighting. The people of Africa instinctively understood that war was not good.

This was civil war for the people of Africa, a theatre of bloodshed and mentally the people were ready for this war in perhaps numerous ways. Many people fighting the war against the United Nations were small children who did not care about life. The young children fighting were kidnapped from their homes and given drugs to numb any feelings or memories of family life. The young boys of Africa were killers, and products of their environments. Many of the young boys before war with the United Nations would roam the streets of their country taking drugs and hanging out in sex brothels.

When the young boys were abducted from their homes, they were beaten and told that their entire families were dead or would be killed if they cried for their family. The young boys were treated like animals. Also, the boys were hit with sticks or whatever else their abductors could find or pick up from the ground. The boys were made to stand in group formation and made to pledge allegiance to their chief advisor and other members of their new group and family.

The young boys were made to sing this song bright and early in the morning: "No Bible today. I am your god. And you don't have your Bible today. The devil has taken my family today. So I'll kill you to bring them back today." Many of the young boys were beaten so severely during their break-in period, consequently causing many of the boys to die. Many of the boys could not stand on their feet, and because of that the boys consequently were murdered by their peers.

The young killers were blindfolded and handed large assault rifles and told to squeeze their weapons triggers, and kill the people who have killed their mothers, brothers, fathers, and sisters. After the shootings, the young boys were ordered to pull their blindfolds from around their faces, so that they may see the people who have killed their family members. When the young killers pulled their blind folds from their faces, they witnessed the people they had killed. The people whom the young boys killed were other severely beaten and sick children from their kidnapped groups. After the beaten and sick were killed, their killers loudly laughed and cheered each other. One of the young boys who killed his sick group mates was asked about his feelings of killing someone that was close to him. The young boy replied, "My friend was sick or dying, so I killed him, and now he suffers no more pain."

Back to the civil war, the United Nations was losing badly and had began to retreat to safer barricaded perimeters. They began to lose the battle for their belief of not wanting to kill children. A group of Africans have pinned down a group of troops from the United Nations behind a vacant building. The troops have used all their supplies and could not reach their perimeter in time to reload on ammunition. There were eight group members total hiding behind the building. The group decided to dig themselves a passage way underneath the building with their hand and portable shovels that certain group members brought along.

The shooting from the approaching Africans was getting closer and closer each passing second, so the troops dug urgently for shelter. They dug a small hole the size of a small child under the building. The troops screamed profanity to each other and demanded that the person digging dig faster. The leading digger broke free more ground from under the building creating a space for himself to fit through. Quickly as the head digger registered that the space he has dug was large enough for him to fit through, he gratefully jumped through.

Troop members also followed behind the head digger and jump under the abandoned building crawling furthest as possible away from the crawl entry which they created. All troop members were safe temporarily as they hid under this old and weather-damaged structure. Troop members pulled from their backpacks flashlights so they could see the ground which they crawl on searching for better areas to hide from the killer Africans.

All troop members pulled from their packs their flashlights. They saw many rusted pipes under the building, and rats moving freely up and down them. Surprisingly under this old building was very vast, all eight of the troop's spun toward the entryway, waiting for the Africans that trapped them behind the building, the troops pulled any type of tool they perhaps could use for weapons. Three of the eight troops had German long-bladed pig skinning knives and were ready to defend their lives.

Meanwhile, the Africans continued to shoot outside wildly in many directions, warning any one around that a death threat was in the area. A path of death was the Africans' way of marking their territory, before their approaches. Many native people ran furiously through the streets of the country with their hands and arms above their heads for the purpose of not getting shot in the head without trying to protect themselves. Many of the people who ran the streets were scared of the war. Many people had jobs like peanut seller, and sold the fruits of their labor, in nearby town grocery squares.

Naked, abandoned children roamed the streets with wild gunfire blowing over their heads. Seventy percent of the country suffered from poverty. The main source of income was firewood and their food to eat was the wild fruit of the land. Children's classrooms were held outside in some type of cool, open space. Terrifying to the troops a pair of small legs stopped in front of the troops' entranceway.

The troops are nervous and watched the young pair of legs closely as they stood outside the whole's entrance. Some of the troops prayed to their God for chances to see their family again, as they were afraid of their rivals killing them first. The pair of legs turned directly in front of the hole and bent down. It was a very young boy about the age of ten years old. The young boy looked under the building trying to see if he could see something. However, the young boy could not so he got himself up from the ground and stood up running away.

One of the eight soldiers whipped the sweat from his upper head, and others thanked their creator for not letting them die today. The soldiers were blinded from the total darkness from under the rat-infested building and cannot see one another. However, the light from outside shined in the whole one yard. The soldiers all continued to pause and wait out any ambush attempts from the African people outside.

The soldiers wait for thirty minutes before they moved toward the light of the hole. A soldier pulls his flashlight from under his chest and flashed the light up at the floor signaling his peers that he will move first for the entrance of the hole and exit first. The soldier made his move and crawled as fast as possible for the hole, the rest of the soldiers following closely behind. The leading soldier made it to the entranceway very cautiously before entering into the light that shined in the hole and underneath the building.

Having enough courage, the leading soldier entered into the light of the hole. He looked around very slowly as he listened to any type of movement or heavy breathing from outside. The soldier was very nervous and scared to stick his head outside the hole to check for enemy targets. Inch by inch, the soldier made his attempt further and further closer toward to the exit. He made it to the exit, calmly reaching it with the top of his head. The soldier's eyes have not yet made it outside the hole to where he can see anything, instead the soldier stared up outside the hole but at the moment, he can only see the sky. He inched further and now he could see outside the hole entirely, making eye contact from the barrel of a very dark and angry African man, who lay on the ground with his automatic weapon pointed at the soldier's head.

The very dark African man very slowly with his free hand, gestured the soldier out the hole. The soldier obeyed and climbed from the hole, as instructed very slowly with other members following behind the first soldier, before they could see what beholds them outside. Two soldiers followed behind the first soldier and now they stood outside the hole with their hands above their head. A fourth soldier who followed behind the third soldier saw what laid outside and immediately stopped and backed away from the entrance, alarming the remaining four soldiers as they all moved quickly from the hole entrance.

Six African men ambushed the soldiers very patiently as two of them laid on their stomachs outside the whole waiting on the troops from the United Nations. The three soldiers were quickly guarded by the four African soldiers, who held automatic weapons pointed at them. The African soldiers asked the troops from the United Nations in their broken English language if there were anyone else down there. The troops replied no. The African soldier asked once again to the troops if there were any other person under the building.

The African soldier had three stripes on his uniform stating that he was a commander and chief of his group of men. The commander signaled one of his men forward and ordered him to go get some gas from their vehicle inside their emergency gas tanks. The drums required two men to retrieve them from the trucks. The tanks weighed over seventy-five pounds. The men retrieved the gas from the vehicle and presented the drums, as instructed by his commander.

The three troops looked at each other in no hurry as they looked in each other's eyes for sign of Fright of being burned alive. The commander asked the three troops if they understood what the gas was for and the troops replied they did not know. The commander laughed and told the men that he believed that they can think of some sort of reason that the gas could be used for. The commander next turned to one of his officers, and the officer knew to make the troops drop to their knees. One of the three troops spoke loudly, replying, "I will tell you who's under there!"

The commander replies, "Don't worry, little men. The gas is not for you, it's for your friends!" The commander ordered his men to pour the gas under the building and set fire to the flammable substance. The men did what their commander asked of them. The liquid was set on fire and muffled screams came from under the building.

The military troops from the United Nations started screaming and crawling from under the abandoned building, screaming from the pain. The African soldiers took shots at the troops, killing them and putting an end to their suffering. The commander spoke: stop shooting the troops and let them suffer for what they have done to the mother land of the world. However, the three troops from the United Nations started to cry from the killing of their peers and the fact that they were soon to follow the same faith!

Only three of the troops left from under the building and were shot while on fire and the other two remaining troops were made to suffer before dying of a painful death. The three remaining troops were asked how they wished to die and the men did not reply. The commander ordered his men to line up in a straight line with their weapons ready for fire on the United Nations troops. The soldiers lined up following their commanders orders and lined up ready to kill the troops upon permission.

The three men looked up toward the sky and began to speak with their Lord and Savior but the troops have been warned from the soldiers from Africa, "that no Bible exists today." The soldiers pulled their weapons from the ground and pointed them at the troops and began to laugh at the troop as tears of death rolled down the men's faces. The troops looked at each other for the last time of their lives, before the African soldiers opened fire on them.

The troop's bodies were beaten to pieces from the automatic weapon fire of the Africans guns. One of the troop's head was blown wide open from a fifty-five grain bullet. The troop head popped open so quickly that the blood exploded from the wound caused by the bullet. The other two troops were shot multiple times in the upper chest and face area, until they hit the ground alongside the first troop that received the head womb.

Different parts of the takeover revealed United Nation troops being sexually assaulted and having their genitals severed off by the African people once they were captured. Rocket launcher smoke filled the air commonly for the last thirty odd days since the queen began taking over Earth. United Nations snipers, a pair of two, pluck off a group of rebels who have just blown up a tank with a rocket launcher from a rooftop. The men were celebrating when the snipers took their shots.

The attempted takeover of Africa was no good and the people of the country refused to surrender and follow behind a woman. Young boys were spotted by the snipers running across a street in the war and death-infested town with weapons larger than they were. The boys ran inside a vacant building and prepared themselves to kill anyone unexpected and from the United Nations. The boys were observed moving around in the large twenty-story building. The boys made their way up to the fifth floor of the establishment and set up their weapons to make kill shots on any person of foreign blood.

The snipers took shots at one of the boys and killed him instantly from a neck wound. The other remaining boy did not understand what had happened yet, and he was unaware that his friend stood behind him holding his neck whispering how he wanted his mother. One of the snipers detected from his telescopes lens located at the top of his long range rifle the reflection was spotted from an African sniper who opened fire on the sniper from the United Nations.

A man holding a rocket launcher standing on the side of the African sniper decided to release one of his rockets on the snipers from the United Nations, making sure that no uncertainties existed from a threat being eliminated. The rooftop that supported the sniper was partially blown to pieces, the falling debris from the roof hit a couple women running with their children. However, the debris hit one of the women and she never stopped to notice a tennis ball size brick hit the surface of her head. Instead, she ran faster.

Satellite images were received by Sara' from Ms. Thomas. Thomas saw the fax machine light flashing and retrieved the papers from the machine. Reports came in notifying

Ms. Leon that five hundred thousand United Nations troops have lost their lives trying to siege and control the Blinder. Women also held weapons and have killed troops from overseas.

Joining nation's dear wish not to be the first to complain to the queen of losing so many men. Sara' was notified of the lives lost, from electric signals inside the chips of her troops, her new children from earth. Sara' looked at Ms. Thomas from her living room and penetrated her mind, immediately understanding what the paper read. Sara' walked in Thomas's direction, walking up to her and reaching for her hands. She hugged Ms. Thomas, teleporting both of them inside the White House.

Sara' and Thomas both ported inside the president's office terrifying him as he crawled under his desk and begun to cry tears of freight. Ms. Thomas walked over and sat at the president's desk and picked up his office phone and ordered all troops to retreat from Africa immediately. Satellite images showed the United Nations backing out of the country respectfully as Sara' ordered.

Walking over to Thomas, Sara' touched her head showing her an image of love and warmth, and sporadically images of death and destruction took hold of Thomas, making her grab both of Sara''s arms as Sara' held her head inside her large hand. The president looked up at what was taking place and stopped crying in hopes that Sara' did not notice him hiding under the desk in his office; Sara' looked down at the president after she removed her hands from Thomas's head and vanished!

APPEARS IN AFRICA!

Sara' appeared in Africa, walking the bloody and death-infested roads, observing the dead scattered amongst the land from the war of the nations. Many people from both sides fighting did not notice Sara' for some time, due to the excitement from the war. Many African people sped past her looking back taking occasional glances at the queen standing on their land. An old woman tried her best to run the dangerous streets of her country, so she could find some type of safe haven for herself, a place to escape from the loose bullets. However, Sara' continued her walk up this road of this country, taking in all she wished before her anger erupted. The old woman found her haven and hid herself in an abandoned apartment stairwell when she spotted Sara' from her cover. She shouted, "You are the queen of death!"

Other African people running past Sara' and the old woman who was the first to notice her slowed their pace and paid better attention to the old woman and the tall, beautiful lady walking down the road of their town. A group of rebels have driven up the road and almost hit the group who slowed down to get a better look at Sara' and the queen of earth with their truck. The troops continued to run, and left the town aware of the murders that will take place on anyone caught in the queen's wrath.

The rebels jumped from the truck firing their weapons and screaming the words: "We want peace." One of the men ran in front of Sara', not aware of her tall height. The rebel made gestures of sexual nature of himself riding an invisible horse in front of Sara'. The queen of earth stopped her walk and softly told the man to come to her. The man obeyed willingly and Sara' held her arm forward and the man reached grabbing Sara''s hand and kissing it.

After kissing the queen's hand, the rebel held his head up from her hand and quickly stood upright with a look of panic. The rebel stood up straight looking around with his mouth open wide as if he wanted to make a statement but forgot what he wanted to say. The man's skin started to tighten, beginning at the rebel's feet first. Now the rebel's leg started to give him trouble as he screamed loud and painfully. The man was beginning to turn into leather very quickly. Both his legs have turned and so have the left side of his face and fingers.

Sara' stood before the man and whispered, "I don't love you anymore!" The man stood straight up and gasped for air and tried to shout but he could not. His mouth tightened shut and his dying life was leaving his body. The now dead rebel's other group mates saw what happened to their friend and group brother. Fear jumped into the surviving rebels, making them and other African onlookers who witnessed the strange killing of the rebel flee to the bush hiding with the wild animals of their land. People of many fled as if this country and its people understood who Sara' was. A large number of people had handicaps, such as missing limbs and women. Many of them we're missing breast. However, it appeared they all run the same speed—toward the jungle!

The trees of the jungle were tall, and the terrain was very rugged. The trees had large rope type vines hanging from the trees that certain monkeys and apes hung from them. Suddenly the jungle was very quiet. Wildlife of all breeds importantly zeroed in on the approaching crowds. The jungle floor shook, as the fleeing crowd approached closer and entered the forrest.

Birds departed from the treetops, as some of the people entering the jungle brushed up against some of the trees disturbing the animals. Some women of the approaching crowd exceeded more than five children and were single parents because many of the women's husbands have been killed or kidnapped and made slaves to work the diamond ponds. The men were made to stand in large ponds of water wearing very little clothing and in some cases naked.

Most of the tree animals fled deeper into the jungle, fearing the rumble from the approaching crowd. People were screaming for God and asking the Lord to spare their lives. The African people continuously entered and ran further into the forest with the wild animals, and instinctively the people naturally understood to quiet themselves with the animals.

Sara' spotted the crowd and approached the people intensely as she walked up the road slightly jogging. Some elder men of the crowds urged the women to keep their small babies quiet or they would have to murder their children. Sara' continued to motion forward in the direction of the crowds, as she stepped over dead men from America and the United Nations.

Blood puddled from wounds located on corpses' heads. The skulls were smashed in several areas from bullet holes or machete cuts. Sara' stopped herself and appeared to observe the road miles ahead which supported hundreds of dead bodies. Meanwhile, the African people continued to keep surveillance on Sara'. Many people had assault rifles and rocket launchers aimed at the murderer, queen of blood, translated into English.

Sara' stopped and motioned her head from side to side, as if searching for weak areas of the crowd's defense. Many dead bodies lay dead over the scattered road were men, so it would appear that way. Glancing down toward the ground, Sara' noticed a difference with one of the dead corpses lying on the ground. Turning left, Sara' walked up the hill toward this dead person. However, the African people never once took their eyes off the killer. The jungle was full of fear and panic. Sara' had many weapons pointed at her from the people hiding in the jungle. Stepping over many dead men, Sara' continued to move toward whatever captivated her attention.

There were numerous burned and abandoned vehicles also on the road and in ditches located to the left and right sides of the road. The ditches were each three feet deep in water on each side, which continued to flow further down its path connecting into one massive funnel of deadly, toxic river sewage water that was created from the native people dumping human waste into the stream.

Sara' fondly reached her purpose and kneeled down and wiped the blood off the corpse's face that was different from the other dead bodies and removed the helmet from the body's head. Sara' noticed the long hair that fell from under the helmet. She continued to wipe away the blood and dirt from the body's face. Semblances of the corpse's face appeared more and more of a woman, and shockingly it was a woman.

The woman was a nurse who aided wounded soldiers on the battlefield. The nurse was shot twice in the head from long range fire because the entire left side of the dead woman's head was missing. The dead nurse upset Sara', making her stand up and boldly face the crowd. Sara' began to walk off the dirt road and down into the ditch.

Sara' entered and walked through the murky water, stalking the crowd. The people observed Sara' wearily through thick brushes and from behind tree trunks. Many of the men pointed loaded weapons at Sara', anticipating an attack. Sara' walked from the ditch, never taking her large eyes off the crowd in the Forrest. A baby cried out loud from the thick Forrest, making Sara''s head redirect her direction.

People surrounded the crying baby and mother looked at the mother with worried looks on their faces. The mother grabbed her baby's mouths, trying to quiet her daughter as she looked at members of her group with sweat and tears in her eyes. People have chosen to remove themselves from the crying baby and crept off to other parts of the jungle. The old man who warned the women earlier of quieting their babies now stalked this particular mother and crying child. The old man had a rock hammer in his hand. The tool was made for cutting wild meat in the bush. The old man was a very skilled hunter and now moved slowly toward the mother and baby.

The old hunter was careful not to step on anything that would make noise and alert the mother of the crying baby. The old man directed himself around people trying to get within striking range of the baby. The old man wished to kill the baby for the better good of the large group of people. The woman held her upset baby tightly against her breast, appearing to smother the child. The old man moved quickly and struck the baby once. The mother had closed her eyes as a signal of relieving stress and did not see the old hunter strike her child.

The baby never cried again after she was struck in the head. Instead blood shot from the little girl's head like a high-pressure water gun. Opening back her eyes, the mother of the little girl was Unaware of her daughter's death while in her arms and screamed out loud. A second man from the group of people watched the woman attempting to take in air for the purpose of keeping up the reckless commotion that was considered hazardous toward the larger percentage of the group. This smaller man watched the mother very closely as he watched the woman open her mouth as wide as possible before he gripped his machete tightly before running forward toward the woman considering he was just feet from the grieving mother. The man lifted the weapon high into the air, assuring the machete reaches maximum cutting power as the man swung the blade back down and across the woman's throat, decapitating the woman's head from her surprised and dying body.

The woman's surprised body fought back ferociously for life as it was aware that life was leaving from it. The body tried clenching the air around it only to fall toward the rich soil of Africa, empty handed. Different men and women who witnessed what happened to the woman and the crying child grabbed their children tight against their bodies. Meanwhile, Sara' continued to stalk up the hill after the people who have killed many Americans and other United Nation members.

Sara' pranced up the hill toward her victims, eager for the sacrifice of the people of this land. The queen of earth desperately sought revenge for the lady nurse who was killed and lying on the side of the road. Many people possessed their weapons tightly in their hands. However, no one wanted to be the first individual to squeeze the trigger. The people were afraid that Sara' would surely attack their group of people if they fired shots first at the queen. Sara' positioned herself in the position of a large jungle cat, supporting herself on all four limbs.

Earth's new queen ran up the hill, faster and faster than seconds before headed after her targets. A young boy, about the age of sixteen, fired shots on the earth's new queen with his eyes closed shut. Sara' increased her acceleration noticeably toward the person firing shots at her. She took twenty-foot leaps!

Weapon fire rang out wildly and all the Africans shot and screamed. The people will kill the murderer if they only understood how. No one has figured out a way to stop the queen or her omnipresence. Sara' leapt from behind tree trunks and large rocks in the field. The field was covered with dead bodies, alone and stranded with no burial or family to claim them. Sara' never stopped her chase after the people. Suddenly, the queen stopped her pursuit and stood in one place, standing amongst the dead bodies lying in the fields.

Thousands of bullets flew through the air and in Sara''s direction. Bullets hit trees and pierced leaves and birds that remained in the area. The forest was filled with witches and warlords who carried machetes, and war paint that covered their entire bodies. The people of Africa believed that bullets could not pierce their flesh during war because of religious beliefs. However, their fight was for the better good of the bloodline of their people.

Military helicopters from foreign nations circled above the jungle and recorded the destruction of the people of Africa. Small ponds of blood stained much of the ground in the fields and areas surrounding the jungle where the people hid. Looking through the monitor inside the helicopter, smoke rose high into the air from weapon fire, leaving the cover of the trees.

Things happened so quickly and the bullets moved toward Sara' at the speed of three thousand feet per second due to no wind resistance. African women also pulled their triggers in the direction of Sara'. The helicopter recording the destruction was fired upon and was critically wounded as the machine burst into flames, crashing sixty yards behind Sara'. The queen never looked behind her at the crashed helicopter. However, she continued to stare down at the deceased corpses that cluttered the bloody field.

Sara' continued to hold her hand forward, stopping the bullets from making contact with her. One of the corpses that Sara' looked at, the eyes began to twitch. The dead corpse was a troop from the United Nations. Sara' opened her mouth and spoke to the dead soldier, uttering the words, "Get up, my dead child, and go eat the flesh of the people, who smells of the odor of the land."

The troop completely opened his milky color eyes as he rose to his feet, and now he looked the queen in her eyes, acknowledging that he understood her. However, gunfire still dominated the sound of the day and the African people hiding in the jungle fired their weapons harder than ever before in their lives at the queen. The people of Africa who hid in the jungle question why their bullets were not hitting the murderer.

More dead troops rose and surrounded Sara', making a circle around her creating a wall of bodies. The gunfire ceased and the native people witnessed the troops rise to their feet. Some native people cried, "The queen makes the dead disobey God, and return to his earth!" Sara' placed her arm down to her side once the firing had stopped completely.

Sara' told the dead African soldiers and rebels to rise up also. People who witnessed the dead rise began to fall to their hand and knees and cry out loud for their dead native brothers and sisters to rest in peace. Voodoo priests and witch doctors also fell toward the ground and looked up toward the sky for answers from above.

The battlefield was quiet except for the cries of the people. Sara' demanded her dead to move into the jungle and feed on the Africans. The dead troops moved forward rapidly, moving after the people. Sara' walked behind her cannibals slowly. The sun had started to end its shift for the day, causing people to run for shelter fearing that Sara' and her dead will become more powerful during the cover of full darkness.

The dead entered the jungle and stalked the people very cautiously. One of the dead troops stumbled on a decapitated women and dead baby. The troop knelt down and picked up the head of the women and began to eat the head. A dead rebel walked beside the troop from the United Nations and knelt down and picked up the baby and looked at the child and then began to eat the dead baby's stomach.

Screams left the jungle from man and women alike. A pregnant woman was caught and attacked by Sara"s dead army. The dead attacked the woman as she fell to the ground and began kicking the dead. The pregnant woman kicked her legs rapidly in the air trying to protect herself when one of the dead retrieved her airborne leg and began eating it. The woman screamed for mercy. However, the dead showed no emotion as they looked the dying woman in her face as they continued to feed on her weak and fragile body. One of the dead positioned himself toward the woman's head as he pulled it from her pale body.

Sara' entered the jungle slowly, observing death and cannibalism of UNliving and dead people, Sara' watched death construct itself and multiply in numbers. She spoke very lowly and told the newly dead to feed on their brothers and sisters! Gunfire sounded in the air again as the African people took desperate stands to defend themselves from the queen's death wish on them.

Sara' approached her dead eating the pregnant woman. She looked at them and they the same to her. The dead understood the queens nonverbal communications, and left the corpse. They walked deeper into the jungle after the people. The dead continued to increase in numbers as body parts of the Africans were littered throughout the land. There were thousands of dead that lurked in the dark searching for victims.

The queen of earth continued her walk through the jungle, listening for the sound of control and surrender. A mother hid her two small children under bushes and burnt brush from the forest. The mother hoped that her children would be safer without her attracting attention to her children. The mother told her small daughters to quiet themselves and answer to no one but their mother. The mother told her crying children that she would be back for them during sunrise the very next day.

Newly dead supporters of the queen noticed the smell of undead flesh and followed the smell's direction. The dead looked up in the sky as they sniffed the air for stronger odor trails. One of the little girls accidently kicked a piece of the bush which she hid under, which caught the attention of a dead half-eaten woman. The women approached closer toward the little girls as they both closed their eyes hoping that they were dreaming.

The two little girls opened their eyes only to have the dead woman crawling on the ground before them trying to enter their hidden area. The little African girls screamed loudly and ran from their hiding spot. Sara' heard the two girls and walked in the direction of the screaming children very slowly. The dead chased after the two little children. The children ran as quickly as their seven- and six-year-old legs could travel them. The girls ran through many bushes trying to outmaneuver their assailants.

Meanwhile, many of the surviving African people fled from the jungle, and back into the main area of their city where many dead members from both sides filled the streets. Also, fire consumed many of the buildings and homes surrounding the overtaken city. The president of the country of Africa hid his wife and children safely from danger and made plains to meet the queen, even if it cost him his own life. The president's wife begged him to not leave her and their five children and to let things be as they were.

The leader of the country kissed his family and told them that it was important they understand he must do this for the better good for his countrymen and women. Nevertheless, the two little girls continued to run for their young and precious lives from the dead that followed the queen's commands. Tears and dirt covered the faces of the two small children.

The children ran through their final bush of escape. They entered the large bushes and held their heads down, trying to prevent leaves and other hazardous debris from entering their eyes. The oldest sister was the first to make it free from the bushes and continued to run with her head down. The younger sister also made it free from the vegetation and held her head up, looking at what lay before her path of escape. The older sister ran into a person dressed completely in black clothing. She ran into the person's legs and immediately fell to the ground crying as if she's ready to give her young life up and meet her creator.

The younger sister stopped approximately one yard from where her older sister sat. The younger sister looked in the face of the dark person and sat on the ground behind her big sister. However, the dead made it behind the sisters and picked up the smaller sister and smelled her body as if he wished to make sure him and his followers tracked down the correct flesh. The older sister wiped dirt and tears from her young face and looked up in the face of the object blocking her path.

The dark object was Sara' who stood before the sitting children. Sara' looked at the dead who held the younger sister in the air and commanded him to place the child down back on the ground. The queen of earth looked at the children and told them not to cry anymore and that peace will be delivered to their country. Sara' held her hand forward helping the sister to her feet, telling the kids to follow her.

Sara' and the children began to walk past the crowd of dead and exited the forest headed for the city after the larger groups of survivors. The dead and the small children walked behind the queen. The older sister held her smaller sister around the neck and head area escorting her little sister to safety. The dead continue to look at the children with the taste of dead flesh in their mouths.

The queen and the two small children and her sea of dead, leave the forest and enter the main city headed for the capital. The president and a group of armed men searched for the queen by following the path which his countrymen and women ran the opposite direction from. The African president's wife and children looked at their father for the last time ever.

Daybreak warned its arrival from the singing of birds in the tops of tree trunks. Sara' held her left arm forward and the dead ran after the living, seeking to kill them. Many people looked at the streets from abandoned building windows, from overtaken apartment and office building windows. No one dared to shoot at Sara'. Instead, they held their children and other family members tightly and prayed out loudly.

The sun was deep orange breaking through the late night sky and death fouled the air, giving buzzards and other scavenger animals an invisible navigational meal location that is Unseen to humans. Thousands of dead troops and African rebels and soldiers attacked and destroyed any wounded or person unmindful of his or her safety. Sara' walked up the middle of the road in the direction of the president's home.

The queen walked confident. However, murderously humble during her stride up the road in search of the country's reckless leader. Sara"s dead surrounded her on every side. They even crowded the sidewalks, and violated public safety codes of over maximizing public streets. The president of the country himself searched for the queen, hoping that negotiations could be made to save his people and their land. The president's men who chaperoned him were terrified, and three of the ten men ran and fled for their lives.

Sara' spotted the president of the country and his men approaching just yards up ahead. Sara' stopped her walk and the two small children following closely behind the queen stopped also. The dead also gathered around Sara' and the two small children. They left the city sidewalks and abandoned buildings and they even left other dead corpses on the streets they have partially eaten, so they could protect the queen.

The African president himself located the queen up the road. She's surrounded by her army of dead. The president of the country motioned his hands across his chest as if he wished to pray once he spotted Sara'. The sun rose higher, allowing the president and his men to put out their torches and depend on the light from the sun. The dead also spotted the African leader and began to make sounds of dead music!

Sara' ordered the dead to silence themselves by speaking the words, "Rest your mouths!" Thousands of half-eaten bodies stood before the African leader waiting for him to approach hell on earth. The president's men looked in disbelief at the horror up the road. They stopped walking toward the queen and the mob ahead because they were certain that death stood before them.

Different members of the seven remaining men urged the others on, and ensured the others that there was such a small amount of pain during most deaths and today could be the day they all faced the devil in her eye. One of the men from the group told the president that he will lay down his life for the leader of the country. However, the African leader did not reply. He only touched the man on the shoulder and continued to walk forward.

Sara' stood only several yards away from the leader and his approaching men. The smell of death and decay frightened the president and his men even further. They stopped for a short moment before moving and walking again toward Sara'. The president of Africa approached Sara' and looked her in her eyes, weary. He kneeled before the queen and her dead. The president begged for mercy of the men and women of his country.

The African leader's men held their torches with both hands firmly ready for a fight with the dead and Sara' if need be. The dead looked at the men and once again began to make loud noises and appeared to be agitated. The two little girls who stood behind the queen started to cry, catching the attention of the African president. Sara' told the president to rise to his feet and hold her hand, so the president did as the queen commanded.

Sara' asked the leader who his men followed and the president of Africa replied, "My queen, they follow myself and will lose their lives for me."

Sara' replied, "My child, no one follows you," and at that moment, she ordered the dead to feed on her children and the dead surrounded Sara' and the president and his men, creating a tight harness around them in the middle of the road. The men screamed loudly and so did the small children. However, the dead only attacked and ate the seven men of the country. The two children were covered in blood from the notorious attack on the seven men.

The queen never once loosened her grip on the hand of the leader. Instead, she looked him in his face the entire time his men were being eaten. The leader fell back on his knees, asking the Lord to have mercy on his soul, Sara' interrupted the president's prayer by saying, "No one follows you, they only follow me."

The leader quickly replied, "Yes, my dear queen of great mother earth."

The dead have been told to rise and stand before their queen. The dead obeyed Sara' and stood before her and the president of Africa. Sara' spoke to her army of dead and told them that today and time they will be allowed to rest with family, and at that moment the dead begin to look around at each other before falling to the ground only to never rise again and eat flesh.

Sara' asked the African president who he followed, and the leader replied, "You, my mother not from earth," and kissed her hand. Sara' removed her hand from the leader's hands very slowly and looked up into the abandoned windows of the buildings of the capital, and looking at the hidden people in their faces as some of them looked out their windows to witness what was happening in the middle of their streets.

Sara' stood in the middle of the road, surrounded by death and dead bodies. The two small children slowly walked over toward the African president and held him tightly, as they all appeared to comfort each other. By this time, the sun had fully risen and bodies were occupied by scavenger animals and their young. Sara' looked down at the president and children before rising into the sky very slowly as she headed to her secret location only known to her and members of her dead society who helped build her hidden layer.

THE MEETING

After Africa was punished for their disobedience, a meeting took place involving the conquered countries' leaders who lost control to the alien woman. Brazilian, Canadian, America, and the British president, and lastly the president of Africa, participated in the meeting voluntarily in support of their queen.

The meeting took place one mile below the east Pacific Ocean, inside Sara"s underwater lair, the coordinates of the lair are hidden from the general public, do to any outside planet, wishing to apprehend the queen. The leaders arrived inside a high pressurized submarine escorted below the ocean, from a hidden generation of mermaids and mermen. The creatures remained scarcely hidden from humans, as they tried to replenish their nearly extinct race. The leaders aboard the submarine have never witnessed creatures of this sort before. However, they have seen hundred-thousand-year-old cave pictures, painted on walls of numerous caves of the armed mermaids.

The submarine was purposely made of tungsten steal, with an aluminum mixture for the purpose of lighting up the ocean beneath. The sub was designed to reflect any amount of light ten times. There were many mountains beneath the east Pacific Ocean, and the mountains were well lit with special light post, which could sustain the deep water pressure. Many lamps surrounded the hills supplied from the hidden creatures exposing many different mermaid families that occupied the surrounding mountains as residents.

The leaders could not believe their visions of the ocean hills. Everything around the ship was pitch black and terrifying, and so the lights were comforting to the men on the submarine. Sara"s underwater castle began to appear in view, making the leaders open their mouths wide full of amazement. The home was beautiful and had many different levels, and hallways made of special metals and high pressure glass, that could also sustain the ocean's weight.

Sara"s lair was also well lit and the light from her home supported life for many nocturnal sea animals. The nocturnal sea animals have adapted to surviving without light from the earth's suns, so the lights from Sara"s home helped the animals tremendously. Unexpectedly, the leaders grabbed their ears with the palm of their hands attempting to squeeze their hands together, trying to depressurize their heads from the ocean depths.

The mermen and mermaids surrounded the submarine, appearing to understand the leaders' conditions aboard their vessel. The African leader stared out the window of the submarine, as if he had witnessed the creatures before, while the other leaders aboard the submarine began to vomit from ocean sickness. The African leader was not affected as the others. The creatures were soft silver with faint colors of purple and pink mixtures. One of the larger mermen placed both of his hands on the window of the submarine as if he wished to communicate with the African leader.

The president of Africa approached the window of the ship very slowly and consciously toward the merman. Meanwhile, the other leaders now lay on the floor of the submarine, dizzy with vomit covering their faces as they looked up to witness the communication with the leader and the alien fish man. The man's vision now was blurry. However, they remained focused in the direction of the communication attempt of the African president and the merman.

The African leader touched the glass of the underwater vessel, and so did the creature. Hey, boy, what are you doing down here, the African leader question the animal? They both looked deeply into each other's faces with curiosity. The merman had very large eyes which were equipped for low lighting, and nostrils were located on top of the creature's head between the eyes. The creature also appeared capable of breathing air from land and oxygen underneath the water which the creature's body was capable of extracting from the sea water.

The African leader removed his hand from the submarines window very slowly. It appeared he lost his nerves looking into the large creature's eyes. Suddenly the merman appeared to inhale a large mouthful of water. The leader left a heated hand print on the window of the submarine when he removed his hand. The creature exhaled the water from his mouth and made the hand print disappear from the cold blast, of Pacific Ocean water.

Next, there was an intense sound that followed behind the water that startled the African leader. The creature held up both arms with a weapon in his left hand. The weapon was a spear that was used for hunting. The commotion from the creature's excitement aroused the other mermaids and panicked the other leaders aboard the ship.

Just as quick as the ocean sickness struck the leaders, it was over. Now all four leaders stood behind the African leader staring out the window of the submarine, looking at the creature responsible for causing so much ruckus. Meanwhile, the ship continued to drift further down toward the ocean floor, set for Sara"s lair coordinates. The front of the submarine had two very large lights that lit its path fifty feet ahead of the submarine.

The large merman continued to make some sort of war cry, which was quickly drowned out by the view of the underground city, which Sara"s home was part of the community. Many rare species of fish swam in front of the lights of the submarine, seeking heat from the ship's lights—fish such as the goblin shark and also the very large vampire squid whose color was dark as blood.

The merman quickly attacked and chased off the large goblin sharks and gruesome squids. Glancing back at the underwater mountains, there were many reflecting eyes bouncing of the craft's lights. The mermen and mermaids' eyes reflected light, making the creature's vision capable of maximum sight considering the animals lived in an area on earth that sunlight was incapable of reaching. Sara"s home was only yards away from the submarine, and the ocean became lively with life of all types, mermaid and mermen alike. Sperm whales circled the deep ocean floors using their echo locaters, in search of food. Life was abundant one mile below the east pacific, organisms of many feed on a fallen and dead tuna that has reached the seabed.

The ocean was a universe of its own and uncharted by humanity. There also were many active underwater volcanoes that supported a large group of dragon vent lobsters that fed from the volcanoes. It was believed that life on planet earth could only live if supported from the sun and its heat. However, a visit to Sara"s laid proved differently.

The lair ETA was now sixty seconds from connection with the submarine. The craft was a very important utensil for Sara"s home. The mermen halted and let the craft further descend, watching the vessel unite with the earth's queen home. The fish men listened closely for the craft to connect with the lair before swimming off.

The pod was connected from its front end, and pulled through a highly pressurized tunnel that connect to Sara"s home. All the men backed away from the front end of the submarine and headed toward the rear of the vessel. They appeared frightened. The pod began to move forward willingly down the glass tube hallway. The men looked up and noticed nature swimming above their location through the see-through tunnel glass of Sara"s home.

The hallway was well lit as was the mountain where the mermaids and mermen lived. However, the leaders' view of the outside from the tube hallway looked like large, monstrous shadows flying and circling above them. Meanwhile, the submarine continued to move down the hallway, which began to incline upward slightly. The leaders aboard the submarine felt the elevation in their stomachs. Each grabbed the chairs inside the submarine and started to pray.

The view of the hallway suddenly became darkened due to the incline of the ship's travel down the long hallway. The submarine was entirely dark and made from the strongest metal on earth, tungsten. This metal was the color steel grey but reflected well, with the aluminum mixture. The metal was nineteen times denser than water and 70 percent denser than lead. After being pulled down the hallway for a short amount of time, low lighting began to be turned on. There were tens of lights cut on, lighting up the submarine's path. Looking out the front of the submarine, the leaders saw a tall, shadowy figure standing down the long tunnel.

The submarine reached its destination and the tall shadow figure began to walk away and disappeared from the leader's vision. The leaders all looked each other over before making any sound. The president of America chose to be the first to speak up: "Hey, fellas, where did it go? Can anyone see anything? The president of Africa: I believe the figure was our queen.

Completely stopping down the end of the hallway, all the leaders exited the submarine one man at a time. All the leaders now stood outside the submarine inquiring verbally very lowly of their coordinates, when a different figure, much shorter than the previous figure seen before, showed up at the end of the low lighted hallway. The figure spoke: "Gentlemen, follow me, your queen patiently awaits you."

The presidents followed the woman and headed in her direction. The leaders walked down the hallway of Sara"s home and noticed many paintings and pictures of some strange solar system. The pictures appeared more like a map of a strange planet Unknown to earth scientists. There were also pictures of many strange animals and plants hanging in the queen's home.

All the different leaders arrived to their assigned area from Sara''s helper, Ms. Thomas. Thomas invited the leaders inside of a conference room, centered in the middle of Sara' Leon's home. All the men were asked to be seated and wait for the queen of their planet. The leaders obeyed Ms. Thomas and seated themselves as asked. Shortly after sitting down, Sara' entered the room and the leaders stood at attention as a sign of respect for their queen. Hello, my queen, we come as you commanded! Sara' immediately began to instruct the men of the purpose of their visit to her home.

Meanwhile, marine life circled the outside structure of Sara''s home, as the animals desperately enjoyed the heat from the lights of Sara''s underwater lair. The heat from the lights caused many deep ocean marine animals to come within deadly ranges of larger predatory animals. The leaders looked up toward the open ceiling of Sara''s home at the underwater sea life, as the queen of earth continued to instruct the men of their obligations.

Sara' spoke to the leaders of the world by telling the men: men be seated and understand me. You are important, and so are the lives of your fellow country women and men. You are privileged to keep your leadership positions. You men will meet me in the country of Afghanistan, so which my speech should be delivered to the people of the unstable country.

You men have been selected to keep your positions as a sign of trust and beliefs in your abilities. Your purpose under the ocean is to understand that you will follow me around the world until we are complete as a unit. Men, you will head east with your armies and prepare for battle!

Certain countries were told to travel the oceans and other countries were told to travel across foreign countries and to violate their boundary lines. Sara' stopped speaking of anything of importance and asked the men to stand. All the presidents stood themselves as they all looked each other over very carefully. Ms. Thomas interrupted the silence and deep concentration of the presidents by asking the men: Do you understand your queen?

All the presidents acknowledged Ms. Thomas's question, of their comprehension of the meeting and the instructions of Sara', "Yes, we understand you loud and clear, my queen, the leaders simultaneously responded. The president of America chose to speak twice: "my queen, what should we expect from the invaded countries?" "Expect for the nations to not understand my purpose and expect them to destroy your beliefs." Sara': "Go home and enjoy time and life with your families, I cannot promise any life extensions." "My queen, my name is Murphy, the president of Africa. I want to mention that I and my people understand your purpose highly." All the men were told to turn around and head back to the submarine as Ms. Thomas chaperoned them back to Sara''s underwater vehicle.

SUICIDE BOMBER!

Troops entered the country of Afghanistan ahead of the queen for the purpose of securing entranceways and abandoned roads, guaranteeing Sara' a safe entrance into the holy country. Ms. Thomas picked a key location that suited the queen's purpose of delivering her speech. The people of Afghanistan ran rapid with open gunfire around their cities and towns, using weapons that were delivered to them from foreign nations.

There were many different nationalities of people populating this country. The location for Sara"s arrival was the Darul Amen Palace. The structure of the palace had many open windows that were suitable for surveillance of the open city, making it easy for spotting any attempts of sniper fire from any angry nationals, or foreign enemies.

The palace was once a disaster of invading nations and Taliban bombings. The building was refurbished for the need of giving hope of bettering lifestyles of the Afghanistan people. The palace was placed on top of a hilltop, overlooking the capital of the western parts of the Afghanistan capital.

Afghans stood in the garden surrounding the European-style building, awaiting for the new queen of earth. The people wanted to witness Sara' in the flesh. At the east side of the palace stood many soldiers from overseas, and African rebels and soldiers from further south. Ms. Thomas stood on a balcony of the palace overlooking the thousands of people awaiting Sara''s arrival. The garden of the palace was beautiful for five hundred kilometers, giving the palace a feel of heaven on earth. Further looking west, the grass of the palace died gradually and became the color brown with hardship and death. Many bullets and heavy missile projectiles cluttered the dirt and gravel, killing the image of imaginary peace of this country.

Inside the courtyard were many women covered with veils and their heads hanging low toward the ground, honoring the beliefs of their religion and the men of their country. Hundreds of Afghan women participated in the queen's visit, hoping for change and relief of old traditions and customs. The women of Afghanistan wanted to be independent, mentally and physically, of a male-dominant society. The temperature in this country was over one hundred degrees, and the Afghan women began to move their clothing around their sweaty bodies, trying to allow their skin a chance to cool itself off from the heat and perspiration from their hot skin.

The reason for Sara''s appearance in the rocky landscape was to release the women of mental slavery and organized marriage. The volume was loud from the Afghan people shouting and yelling words such as "We are soldiers of Allah," and "The queen will die." Some men also were screaming "Babylon has returned to kill all kings and to take the world for herself."

Large speakers were set up around the perimeter of the palace, making it possible for the queen to be heard. Meanwhile, Ms. Thomas was handed an electronic earpiece that allowed her to speak and be heard from the sea of Afghans. Thomas spoke and uttered, "Hello, women. A new day will make history in your country and your daughters will learn great lessons of you're newly found independence."

Many of the men and women were noticeable confused of the language barrier, between themselves and Ms. Thomas. After Ms. Thomas finished speaking, her words were converted into the Pashto and Dari languages. Both were Indo-European languages spoken by the people. Other languages were Uzbek, Turkmen, Balochi, and Nuristani, which were languages spoken by the majority of the people.

Meanwhile, to the back of the palace, the soldiers were growing restless for the lack of action and murder. Many of the men began to clean and take apart their weapons and their weapon sights, predicting their perfect kill shots of the Afghan people. The African soldiers carried late model AK-47 assault rifles with machetes strapped across their backs.

Unsuspectingly swirls of clouds appeared above the capital of Afghanistan, swirling above the people and cooling down the hot temperature of this part of the country. Everyone present looked up into the sky, unsure of the dark clouds' purpose. Ms. Thomas's speech was interrupted of her Unsureness also. The clouds began to swirl intensely with an unspoken purpose.

People quieted themselves and focused their vision high into the earth's atmosphere. The cloud descended down toward the seas of people slowly until reaching its destination. The tunnel cloud appeared heading in the direction of the balcony where Ms. Thomas stood only feet from the palace balcony. Thomas begun to back away from the entrance of the balcony, slightly worried for her life.

The tunnel cloud sounded like a large freight train riding on frozen metal tracks. The tunnel cloud reached the balcony entrance. The tip of the cloud was entirely pitch black. Afghans began to pray, falling face first into the earth, crying for mercy from Allah. The soldiers from America and other joining nations hid themselves under military vehicles and others ran for shelter inside the palace.

The cloud began to disappear and only the dark shadow remained in the physical appearance of a woman. The figure turned toward Ms. Thomas and appeared to reach an arm forward gesturing the ex-military leader besides itself. Thomas moved forward slowly, unsure of what could happen to her. The tip of the figure's arm began to turn into human flesh.

The figure has entirely transformed itself into flesh, its head last. A very old Afghan ma looked up from the ground, his face covered with dirt. The old man cried the words, "Babylon, we have forsaken you. Please forgive us all, my queen." The figure was Sara'. She extended both arms forward upside down and her palms facing up, as if she held a dead child out over the balcony.

Ms. Thomas removed her earpiece and tried to hands it to Sara'. Sara': "No, my sister, I will not need your device." Sara' overlooked the balcony for some time before she spoke to the people of this country. Everyone present remained silent, absent of words. Sara' spoke delivering her speech to the people of this country, and the world intended.

"Hello, people of planet earth. I am the Queen of Kingdoms. I will never be a widow, because I'm dominant over men. I will never suffer as you women of Earth. I will never lose any child to death! A new beginning has fallen on you, humans of my new home. I'm your mother and you people are my children. I have made the people of Africa my children also. I have stricken my children of Africa, and spared no rod of mercy.

"My children, we must venture forward and become one body and prepare for dominance over numerous solar systems. We must remove religion and blind faith and be sure of our destiny. I will remove all outside influences from your country and make planet earth efficiently stronger. Men have confused the world and have intervened in foreign affairs. Men have benefited from other's pains. However, I will send my children home out of their neighbor's yard.

"I will replace your leaders with leaders of my own. My leaders will be manageable for the sake of planet earth. Invading nations will prey on your weakness of religion, and agree with you, my children, and wish to destroy any signs of peace. Every foreign face must leave any neighboring country and go home immediately. People of earth, your wars are meaningless. My children, you have stepped over boundaries that are not of your own. We must become one and dominate solar systems."

All women, my speech has ended; however, I ask you women, to pick yourselves from the ground and wipe the dirt and dust from your clothing. "Your sister and queen commands this of you!" The speech was electrifying and caused many women to look down at the soil deeply in thought of what they have just heard from the woman from the planet Adamen.

The Afghan women looked around at each other, Unsure if they should follow Sara"s orders. Oddly around the sea of people, women began to rise on their feet looking at the large speaker boxes surrounding the garden, and palace rocky hillsides. Some men of the country grabbed their wives and teenage daughter's arms forcefully, in disagreement of their queen's orders, and commands of their wives and daughters.

Secondly, Sara' asked the Afghan women: sisters, remove your veils. Suddenly more women stood on their feet at attention, removing the veils from around their hot faces, on their way up from the moist ground and dirt. Sara' angered fellow countrymen, and their neighbors. The men of Afghanistan also began to rise on their feet screaming at the women from their country in their native language for their disobedience of their religion and moral beliefs, by following the queen's orders.

The Afghan men screamed loudly and proudly encouraging each other, replying the words, "Holy war!" The men began tearing off their clothing and kicking the ground, highly upset of the disrespect from their wives and daughters. Sara' continued to speak with the Afghan women, promising the women education alongside the men of their country.

Sara' further spoke notifying the Afghanistan people how she wished to help the people of their land with outside help, selected from her stable of noblemen and women. However, the Afghan men refused the queen's assistance. Strangely, Sara' closed her large eyes and appeared to be in some type of hypnotic trance. Sara' detected several men and women in the crowd of people hiding explosives under their clothing.

The men and women hiding the explosives under their clothing were suicide bombers who were secretly planning a murderous attempt on earth's new queen. Sara' only wished to keep the peace in the holy city, and stop the fighting in the country. Sara' held out both her arms forward as if taking hold of a large ball. She elevated the bombers high into the earth's atmosphere.

People begun running and yelling from the bombers being lifted into the air. "Allah Akbar," meaning, "God is greater." Sara''s troops left the east side of the building, headed toward the west side of the palace ready to aid their queen, and destroy anything or person she wished. The bombers were huddled close together in the air, they grabbed at each other terrified of their elevation, high above the ground. Several of the suicide bombers, women, loudly asked Sara' to forgive them, and if they may have another chance.

People from the crowd looked up and pointed in the direction of the bombers, continuing to repeat the words, "Allah Akbar." The queen's troops arrived in front of the palace, pumped up full of adrenalin ready for the death of the Afghan people. Many of Sara''s soldiers screamed loudly with the people locked inside their rifles and automatic weapons scopes. They screamed, "Surrender or be destroyed!"

Other troops of the queen were not as pumped up as their partners, and they were able to focus on the large group of people suspended in the air screaming for their lives. Sara' softly whispered, and her words were heard by the bombers very clearly, as if she spoke directly in front of them. Sara' mumbled the words, "This is the day and time I will have you die for me."

After Sara' completed her soft spoken sentence, an explosion interrupts her troop's kill shot and knocked many people to the ground, temporarily blinded and deaf from the dangerous explosion! Fire, blood, and metal fragments went everywhere from the bombers being detonated by the queen. People were covered in hazardous waste, such as internal organs, waste, feces, and many different diseases that could manifest into deadly killers from such human waste.

Meanwhile, the explosion from the suicide bombers was seen for many miles from the capital of Afghanistan. The explosion left a large black cloud in the sky, and blood fell from the air in the form of rain drops. People were now running frantically around the place in complete disorder, screaming for their lives.

Many of the Afghan men ran up the hills and mountains surrounding the palace where they felt comfortable fighting their holy war against Sara'. Expectantly, Afghan men already populated the mountains neighboring the place, aware and knowing of the disagreement with Sara' that the country men predicted to have with the queen.

However, RPG missile fire left from the direction of the surrounding mountains, targeted for the balcony where Sara' stood. The rockets aim and missile projectiles were not accurate over three hundred meters, causing the missiles to strike many of the Afghan men and women who stood directly below the balcony. Sara' never made an attempt to prevent the missile fire from attempting to strike her or the people who stood before her, as if she understood the proper calculations of the RPG missile range limitations.

Sara''s troops opened up with live and destructive ammunition, killing many of the Afghan people effortlessly.

However, many of the women of the country all ran in the same direction, leaving the men of their country to face their queen and sister alone. Ms. Thomas now stood beside the queen as she also looked at the number of bodies lying in the dirt from alien and friendly weapon fire. Bullets hit their vulnerable bodies giving them the appearance of over killed victims of horrible crimes.

The African troops were vicious. They were more murderous than any other part of Sara"s army. The African troops and rebels ran through the crowds of Afghan people shooting through the crowd and not aiming for a particular person. The African troops just wanted to kill and chop bodies into pieces. The American troops preferred to fight this holy war from long range were they were most comfortable killing down the long barrels of their high-tech military rifles.

Troops from the Brittan side arrived on both sides of the palace aiming for the hills and mountains which many of the people from this rocky landscape hid and shot their missiles from, trying to kill anyone from foreign lands, even if it meant killing thousands of their own men and women. Britain's troop's occupied military tanks and pointed their vehicles' weapon toward the hills and mountains and began letting loose destruction by blowing loose chunks of the mountains and hillside surrounding the palace and killing dozens of Afghanistan resistance from the surrounding mountains, which was struck by the Brit's military tanks.

The smell of gunpowder filled the air making it difficult to properly identify each individual's enemy. Sara' importantly looked at her children settling matters between one another as if she understood that her children must solve matters between themselves before she must intervene. Ms. Thomas turned her head slightly and looked at Sara' out of the corner of her eye, as she backed away careful from Sara'. Thomas appeared intimidated of the queen as she understood how the earth's queen can become unpredictable.

Thomas stepped on a soldier's foot from America, who was guarding the balcony from UNwanted guests. Thomas caught herself from further stepping on whatever the object was under her foot and looked behind to see who stood directly behind her. Sara' turned her head slightly and looked at the troop from America and Ms. Thomas behind her, as if the queen had eyes in the back of her head. The troop motioned his head up and down very cautiously, letting Ms. Thomas aware that he understood her intimidations of Sara'.

Meanwhile, hundreds of lives have been lost and people lay on the ground dead or wounded from the exchange of weapons fire. Surrounding countries watched the murder of this land and made the proper preparations toward their country's defense. Russia believed that death before dishonor of their country would be appropriate.

Other countries such as Japan, China, and North and South Korea established communications amongst themselves as they wished to achieve a positive resolution for the best predicament for the men and women of their country. Many people from these countries rioted and protested boldly in the streets of their countries as they demanded protection from their country's government from this woman not of the Milky Way system.

However, back in Afghanistan, many innocent people lost their lives and Sara' witnessed enough fighting amongst her children and held her hands forward back over the balcony and clapped her hands together, creating micro sonic waves that caused her troops and their enemies alike to fall to the floor and hold their heads. Sara's clapping brought the killing and fighting abruptly to an end between the people on the south central region of Asia.

Everyone who surrounded the palace lay on the ground shell shocked from the sonic sounds created by Sara' Leon. Sara' spoke to her confused children telepathically through their minds, telling her children that no one on the planet earth will become independent of her love or structure. The queen ordered her men to rise to their feet and return to their military vehicles. The battle between the people of this country and Sara''s troops only lasted roughly thirty-two minutes before the fighting was cut short by Sara'.

Sara' turned toward Ms. Thomas and demanded her to send everyone north to Russia. Thomas shook her head up and down, replying yes to her mother and sister. Ms. Thomas turned to a troop from the American nation, and notified the troop of the queen's commands. The troop quickly turned and ran down the stairs of the palace, and gathered his fellow troops for their departure north toward the country of the Russians.

GROUND TROOPS!

Sara' sent her ground troops across land headed north through the countries of China, Kazakhstan, and Mongolia to enter Russia. The president of Africa have sent his most notorious states to aid and assist the world's new queen in the now disobedient country of Russia as well. The troops of Africa left the far south of Afghanistan marching through neighboring states, and terrifying residents in fear of memories of past wars fought in their country.

Meanwhile, America and Canadian troops headed east cutting a path across the Atlantic Ocean inside of specially equipped crew carrier, and high speed submarines. Britain and Brazilian allies joined the Americans and Canadians out at sea, to meet Sara' in Russia. It will take the ships a little under a day to meet their queen in the dangerous country.

African troops ventured as far as Liberia, starting their journey of two and a half weeks by vehicle. However, other African troops could possibly touch the Middle Eastern countries sooner considering the state of Egypt connects to the country of Jordan. However, during the leaders' underwater meeting with Sara', every leader present during the conference agreed to rendezvous in the country of Russia at the same time to force structure on the Russian country. Many country men and women whom resided along the path of Sara''s army fled from any area close to their foreign invaders.

The invaded countries had nothing to worry about. However, the queen's destination was preset already and the invading countries never once looked to the right or left side toward the fearful invaded. The troops only faced straight ahead as they understood the importance of their queen's purpose. Sara' left Afghanistan, crippled and conscious of a higher power on their earth. Many died that day and the country was leaderless and now lived in darkness inside their country.

When Sara' punished the country of Afghanistan, she ordered that the entire electric supply be destroyed. She had many electrical grids blown up and their home of residence burnt to the ground. Electrical grids were an interconnector which delivered power to millions of consumers in various areas around the country. Thousands of Afghan people sat in sacred ashes used for mourning and healing the human spirit after their country was made handicapped by the queen. Numerous fossil fuel plants were also destroyed along with the electric grids, leaving the country no choice but to go without electricity.

Meanwhile, Sara''s troops entered the country of China and now crossed over the weary country's border with no type of threat or resistance. African troops invaded China by walking into the country wildly and obnoxiously aggressive. The Chinese people stepped aside of their approaching invaders and let the terrorists pass through. However, many of the people of China have never seen people such as these before.

The people of Afghanistan soon followed close behind the people of Africa. Sara"s followers never focused any signs of threats to any of the trespassed countries. However, the violated countries, never felt any serious threat either because they understood the queen's purpose of themselves. The country of Russia televised their disobedience publicly and that action will not be tolerated from the "queen."

Emergency alerts went off inside the vehicles headed to aid Sara'. Vehicles from the troops lowered themselves closer to the ground and increased their speeds, as their engines were allowed to feed openly on the special, high octane gas in the vehicles' tanks.

The speed of the cars and tanks were enough to throw the occupants from their machines. Crew carriers headed for Russia were signaled of the emergency response from the queen. The naval carriers rose from the surface of the ocean, letting out their high speed sealifts. The ships headed in high speed toward Sara', shortening their distance between Russia substantially.

Meanwhile, wild donkey and mustang fighters flew overhead the ships, and several schools of bottle nose dolphins. The jets would be the first to assist the queen. However, the troops screamed loud and insanely into the wind and dust that's kicked in the air from the vehicles. African rebels shot their guns in the air as they sang songs of their native language.

While other participants of this ground journey focused on holding on to something grounded in their vehicles so that they would not be thrown from their speeding vehicles.

The sun is airborne, at its high point in the sky on this part of the world and it's estimated they will arrive in the Russian country a few hours before sun set on this part of the world.

The queen will transport her vast armies across many countries toward Russia, from pressure to stop killing mankind. The troops were teleported consecutively from Sara' who fought during her attempts. All armies were in disbelief of the occurrences of moving through countries and ocean borders so swiftly as they shouted and cheered from the miracle. However, the troops of the queen were not fully aware of the emergency at hand.

WATER BATTLE

Sara' teleported from Afghanistan and appeared standing on top of the Bering Sea, walking toward the country of Russia. Emergency evacuation sirens sounded out throughout the country of Russia, notifying the citizens of the queen's arrival. It's summertime out at sea and a storm soon approached, and the ocean water created waves building itself stronger for devastation on anything in it, or close to it.

The queen of earth looked up toward the sky, and lowly spoke: my storm, I command you to wait until after my wrath on the country of Russia. Sara' promised the storm a chance to kill. The storm stood at a distance, obeying the queen and allowing the sky to brighten up from a separation of its dark storm clouds. Sara' turned away from the storm and back toward Russia. Sara' stomped on the ocean water, causing the water to whiplash itself, flattening its large ocean waves.

Meanwhile, Russians sang praises of honor as if the country wished death on itself, before dishonor of surrender. Military weather experts notified upper ranks of personnel in charge of special water tactics concerning the sudden retrieval of the deadly storm. Satellite readings of the storm are also retrieved and specially examined, because of the retrieval of the storm.

Images of Sara' were taken from a large crab boat, trapped from the storm out at sea. The images soon hit the internet and the pictures went viral worldwide. However, it was not long before the Russian government's intel department retrieved reports of the photos and sent them to the Russian minister of defense, who was in charge of the nominal head of the armed forces.

A meeting quickly took place, a cause for war. The members were the general staff who was in charge of the executive body, also the ministry of defense which implemented operations and procedures. Fondly the most important is the "State Duma" who exercised the legislative authority over the ministry of defense. The State Duma's main job description was to make sure that Russia armed forces were ready indefinitely.

A destination was reached due to a majority decision from members of the meeting. Russia decided to battle Sara' on water. Russia came to the choice of striking Sara' with a surprise death blow, of underwater submarine attack since Russia had the largest operation of functional submarines. The submarines were nuclear powered which means the submarines could reach speeds of forty-six kilometers an hour.

The submarine was by far the most advanced machinery which humanity had to offer themselves. The subs remained submerged underwater for most of the year, unless coming up for their scheduled dock appointments, which allowed shipmates a chance to touch land and receive mail from family and friends. There were fifteen submarines circling different parts of the Bering Sea, miles from each other.

The submarines waited and stalked Sara' from below as the captains of the machines shared intel from above on land from special forces. Russian military experts were in a state of disbelief as they watched the class eight storm vacate itself. However, Russian naval ships left docks and prepared for war on the queen of earth. Several destroyers and cruisers rushed for battle as they polluted the air and ocean water from their high performance turbine engines.

It was a total of twenty-four Russian ships in all, ready for murder. Crewmembers aboard the ships were yelling and shouting to one another in an effort to prod themselves on. Also, men aboard the ships screamed profound language as they spotted Sara' in the sight of their telescopes. Crewmen and women ran the decks of their ships, rapidly preparing their ships' aircraft and helicopter division for war.

Sara''s ground troops covered land fast, as they flew their diesel air-powered military tanks and trucks. Six nations in all fly after their new queen as they desperately rush to fight her assaulters. The country of America dispersed a fleet of fighter ships up the north Atlantic, headed for their battle with the queen's resisters as well. Meanwhile, military and rebel groups alike traveled through Asia along with Afghan troops.

Canada and Britain flew the skies at one thousand miles an hour in their mustang and wild-donkey aircrafts. One jet could level a city the size of north Hollywood in two hours. One jet carried fifteen missiles and the missiles themselves reached speeds of twelve hundred miles an hour. The missile were heat and remote controlled from military women and men sitting in specialized war warehouses around the world in numerous countries.

Millions of Russian citizens watched television from their homes as pictures of Sara' standing on the Bering Sea, were shown on their television screens: citizens of Russia, we have photos of the alien women who goes by the title, the queen of Earth. The images were taken out to sea. Sara' stood on the water admiring the responses of her reputation from Russia, as they bring their best hand of war forward. Russian ships pointed high power microphones at Sara''s direction hoping to capture any words from the queen. Sara' sensed the communication attempt from the Russian ships, and spoke the words toward their microphones, "I wish not to kill any more of my children, I only want to number and release you."

Sara' believed that numbering humanity would prevent any unawareness toward terrorism against her new home. She also believed knowing her children's whereabouts would bring her closer to everyone in the world. Sara' also believed that numbering children would cause her to have a personal relationship with them and the world could become one and move forward and prepare for a day when the earth will have to fight for its life.

Sara' continued to speak further, "Ships, go back home and do not battle your queen on water." News cameras of Russia displayed images of death and destruction on people from previous nations that Sara' and her army visited. Citizens of Russia sat at home and jumped from their couches, shouting, "Kill the bloody slut." Meanwhile, the Russian military scrambled wildly on their protective bases in a hurry to board their airplanes and jets. The Russian men and women were ready for their battle and believed in their country's armed forces.

However, Sara' stopped her movement and looked down at the water to watch a family of killer whales that swam near her. The animals were curious about the person standing on top of the ocean water. The whales have not seen such a thing before. A large male orca from the pod looked up at Sara' from under the water as he swam up toward her feet. The animal broke the water gently as he stuck his eye from underneath the ocean water, seeking a better look at the queen. The male orca swam directly underneath Sara', sniffing the water under her feet. Sara' kneeled down and rubbed the large animal, and that friendly communication between Sara' and the large male orca made the other animals curious, as they too swam closer to Sara' and smelled the water under her feet.

The orcas were noticeably excited and happy to interact with Sara'. The animals swam wildly under the water, chasing and tugging on each other's fins. However, the primary large male did not engage in play with his other pod members. He merely stayed in place to be loved by Sara'.

Surveillance teams aboard Russian ships observed the queen of earth interacting with something under the water, and immediately informed their superiors of the interaction with Sara' and the ocean water. Captains of the ships have received the information of Sara''s interactions with the water, and contacted the captains of the fleet of submarines below, notifying them of a possible threat to their vessels and crewmen and women.

The submarines circled under Sara', releasing special cameras that would observe her. The cameras picked up a family of orca whales swimming under the water beneath Sara'. Sara' patted the large male on his back, sending him and his family away from this predicted battle. The animals swam opposite from Sara''s direction and headed west toward the setting sun. Sara' stood up and watched the family of orcas swim away. After watching the animals leave, Sara' turned back toward the Russian country.

Meanwhile, Russian military ships have gained certain positions in front of their soon-to-be queen, and prepared themselves for self-destruction. All high ranking military personnel communicated properly through their strict chain of commands, and all last-minute information was delivered to the State Duma by use of radio or emergency telephone hotline. The State Duma gave orders to the military jets which stood ready for their orders of "Live Hot Fire," the name of the Russian mission.

Russian jets left their bases headed for the queen and attempt of her murder. These were jets of the year 2028 and the jets elevated themselves in the air from a standstill position. Russia released fifty jets in the direction of the queen. The underbellies of the aircraft glowed florescent blue. Russia has received alien technology and leads planet earth in all air battles. The jets headed for Sara' and were twenty miles from battle with the queen.

Sara' looked up and spotted the jets twenty miles out and prepared herself for their destruction. Furthermore, the ships were ready also and aimed their guns at Sara'. Sara' took steps forward even faster in the direction of the fleet of ships even though the ships pointed their large guns at her. Crewmen and women aboard the ships took control of their stations and communicated through radio headsets for the purpose of no errors allowed.

The queen continued to approach the ships, making the captains uncomfortable, causing them to fire their weapons. Bullets and missiles alike headed toward Sara'. Everything was so loud and the air seemed like thunder and would shake a person from many miles away. Sara' motioned both her arms and shoulder high, raising herself in the air. Sara' did not waste any time in becoming the aggressor toward Russian armed forces as she began to run toward them from above.

Russian military jets arrived and released fire toward Sara' from more than a mile out on her as well. Sara' rose higher into the atmosphere quickly and barely dodging contact with one of the missiles from the group of ships. Sara' looked at the group of clutter missiles headed toward her and spoke: turn around and destroy the ones who have sent you. The missile turned around and headed back toward the ships. However, some of the missiles made contact with each other and set off each other's detonators. However, not all the missile were blown up, and a good amount of the missile were successful in following the queen's order. Several ships were hit and taking in water quickly. Smoke rose in the air from some of the ships making the people of Russia at home who were viewing the battle of their country have doubts of defeat early in the fight against Sara'. The whole world viewed the battle also, and were hoping that Russia could pull of something that no one in the entire world seemed to be capable of doing with their present technology.

Sara' remained in the air, awaiting the missiles that left the jets headed toward her. Sara' quickly and oddly started to spin in a circle quickly and repeatedly over and over again, creating an invisible force field of electricity which she pulled from environmental radiation in the atmosphere. The electricity from the force field detonated the missiles from the jets before the missiles could reach one kilometer from Sara'. The missiles reached their detonation zones and blew themselves up, causing a ball of fire that surrounded the queen creating a believable image of Sara' destroyed, and blown to death. Murder was delivered to Sara' Leon by Russia, it would be believed.

The Russian jets passed the queen soon after their missiles struck her. Some of the jets flew through the ball of fire which remained airborne surrounding the queen. The ball of fire burned around Sara' for nearly forty-five seconds, which seemed and felt like an eternity. People not only from Russia but around the world were cheerful and crying with tears of joy because of the thought that Sara' has been defeated. Also, men inside the concentration camps around the world were excited themselves because they believed that departure from the camps would be in their near futures now that the queen was destroyed.

However, Sara''s ground air and sea troops rushed even harder toward the assaulters of the earth's queen to rescue Sara'. Multiple satellite images displayed the Russian country being tied in a noose. Images were shown to the entire world on televisions monitors around the planet. Sara''s troops looked similar to army ants in their attack and kill method to capture Russia. The troops of Sara' had the large country surrounded by air, land, and ocean alike. Death and defeat closed in around Russia.

Troop's began to enter the back side of the Russian country through evaded territories they have invaded to get there. Sara''s troops secured the borders between the countries of Kazakhstan, Mongolia, and China, creating a border of their own made of their soldiers' bodies. The primary purpose of this invasion on the Russian country was the city of Moscow. The president of Russia wanted nothing to do with the resistance toward the queen, alongside his fellow countrymen and women. The president of Russia, however, was not the most powerful official in the country.

Meanwhile, Sara"s air force arrived as she sped up her army's arrival by using her powers to teleport her troops dramatically across nations. The vehicles and planes of the queen were programmed to receive emergency information concerning Sara's stress levels, through special software located in her clothing. Mustang and Wild Donkey jets arrived on the scene to open fire on the Russian jets. The jets from Russia were circling around the smoke which engulfed Sara' inside of it. Everything happened so quickly it was hard to understand. Meanwhile, British and Canadian pilots flew the jets of the queen, releasing deadly rounds of ammunition on the Russians. Sara"s air strike shot down and destroyed many of the Russian jets.

The Wild Donkeys and Mustangs were a twenty-first century military fighter planes, made of materials that reflect radar waves from their enemies. The jets also were more flexible than the Russian jets, giving them the ability to outfly the planes from overseas.

British and Canadian missiles were able to sneak up on Russian planes because of new technology they have received from their queen, called the plastic bomb. The bombs were made from mostly high-tech pressurized plastic, which could substance high speeds at high altitudes. After striking and destroying many of Russia's jets from long range, the smoke began to clear and an object faintly rose itself higher into the sky from the smoke.

Cameras of Russia remained located on the remaining jets of theirs, and focused on the clearing smoke and object whose image was distorted from the clearing smoke. Other jets from the side of Russia focused on the invading Wild Donkeys and Mustangs from their enemies across the seas. The Russians were not aware of the plastic bombs their counterparts possessed across the great Pacific Ocean, and were taken by devastating surprise.

Jets of the queen arrived blasting and not caring for death of another person. Russian naval ships opened fire on the Wild Donkeys and Mustangs. The entire country of Russia zeroed in on the object that floated higher into the sky. A ship of Russia picked up clearly on the image first, as it shot a two-ton missile in the direction of the object. The image was later identified as the queen of earth from Russian intel.

Booms and loud bangs of the Americans ships have broken records of the day, it would seem, as they shot large bullets the size of cannon balls from the barrels of their ships' cannons at the Russians. Sara' herself turned toward the sun at the direction of her ships because their guns were so loud. However, Russia fired back cursing at the Americans and the rest of their imposers as they too returned fire. The sky over the Bering Sea darkened once again, and the storm surrounded the water battle, assuming that its time have come to kill. Sara' placed both her legs together and her arm stretched out as wide as they would go. Sara' began to spin in a circle rapidly, causing the storm to back away from the battle between her children.

Sara' gave the storm directions, "stand away and do nothing, your time will arrive," she spoke as she continued to rise higher into the sky. Naval men and women from both sides of the battle looked into the sky closely as Sara' furthered herself from the UNnecessary darkening of the ocean. The water was deep red because of her children's bloodshed. Ships were hit from both sides and many war planes and debris cluttered the ocean below Sara''s ascent. Sara' stopped her spinning and gently continued to rise outside the atmosphere of the planet earth.

The queen once outside of earth hovered above the battle watching the fight closely from outside the planet. Many planes from both sides circled around different ships from opposite sides as they tried to drop bombs made to sink their enemy's vessels to the dark belly of the ocean. Sharks circled roughly six hundred feet below the surface of the water picking off dead remains of voluntary members of the war above their world of residence. Many soldiers drifted further and further toward their watery graves fatally wounded, and other dying soldiers remained slightly conscious but numb of any pain from their wounds as their bodies has released its own antidote to relieve its suffering of pain.

Airplanes and jets were blown apart from both sides and now began to smack themselves on top of the ocean water, and sinking to the ocean floor. Back on top of the water, one of America's crew destroyers was hit from below and pulled water in fast. People aboard the ship ran around this large vessel with fear of drowning out at sea in their minds. However, the Wild Donkeys and Mustangs put up a tremendous battle against their imposers, as some of the jets were able to fire ammunition and missiles into the Bering Sea at the Russian submarines below.

The submarines below were missed from their upper atmosphere attack from the Donkeys and Mustangs above. However, that did not stop the submarines from continuing firing from below. The submarines were not distracted by the missiles. Sara' watched the battle of her children until a tear formed and ran down her honey-skinned tone face. The tear was confusing because it would appear that the queen's arrival to earth was only to murder and dominate this blue and green world.

Sara' allowed her tear to drop from her face and fall into the atmosphere of earth. Sara' watched her tear fall toward earth and it wasn't long before something else caught her attention out the corner of her eye. What caught the queen's attention was life moving past the other side of the earth. Sara' spotted alien crafts observing parts of her new home without an explanation. The look of empathy left the heart of the queen, and an appearance of fury took its place.

The queen turned from the direction of the alien craft slowly, with her face in the appearance of having troubling thoughts before she angrily warped speed ahead back down toward the Bering Sea. A stream of fire broke through the earth's sky causing the men and women fighting the war below to stop firing their guns and missiles and pay attention to the stream of fire that ripped through the sky. Captains of many ships had high-power binoculars glued to their faces as they watched the stream of fire come closer toward the earth.

War jets and planes from both sides maneuvered themselves miles from the apparent asteroid that intruded through their planet's ozone layer. The jets stopped firing at each other and now flew in circles as they kept their eyes focused on the bright orange flame of fire. However, Sara''s ground troops have now entered the grounds of Russia and immediately opened fire on the innocent men and women who stand in their streets to witness their invaders rip through their city and town streets.

Russian bodies hit the pavement with their eyes forced opened from receiving multiple shots from their invaders. The muscle in the shot body's faces did not retract their eyes, they simply didn't have time to respond to close their eyes to deal with the pain in the dark. Instead, the bodies died instantly with their eyes opened wide and pain free. The troops were angry toward the Russians for harming the queen, and wanted dearly to make the Russian citizens pay for their assault on Sara'.

However, the ground troops never planted themselves in one spot in this country. The troops headed directly for the heart of the fighting. Many buildings were hit from large bullets and have begun to show noticeable sign of structural damage. Many scared Russians laid on the floors of their homes holding love ones and small children. Strangely the streets around the iron country were rather empty and surprising considering this country showed a great deal of public disobedience toward their destined queen.

The fire continued to burn bright in the sky, making the rebels and other ground troop members direction naturally sought after. Russia's entire sky burned a deep orange color because of the flame of fire that broke through Russia's part of the earth. Meanwhile, it was quickly assumed that this country figured out that the queen could not be stopped during their early fight for freedom and disobedience with her.

Buildings continued to break apart and crumble and windows shattered from bullet holes. The president of

Russia and many important members of the great country stand in their secret locations focused closely on the water battle and the fire in their sky. Back out at sea, the submarines have taken full advantage of the ceasefire as they continued to fire on their enemies, sinking two more ships from over the great Atlantic.

The fire finished lighting up the sky and now chose to hit the water, hiding itself under the sea. The queen hit the ocean surface with such force that instant hundred-foot waves were created. The large waves pushed naval ships back from each other by considerable yardage. People aboard the ships hit the decks trying to latch hold of anything they could to prevent from being tossed around their ships, because the waves were a threat of capsizing their vessels.

Sara' headed for the floor of the sea, spinning on her way toward the bottom causing a massive whirlpool. The queen had a look of pity on her face even though she currently was under the water. Earth's queen spun with all her might as the mouth of the whirlpool grew rapidly, pulling ships toward the mouth of it. Also submarines under the water began to be pulled toward the neck of the whirlpool and some of the submarines tried to boost their engines to flee. A destroyer from Russia fell prey to Sara's funnel of water and tried hard to exit the first ring of the whirl pool. The ship exhaled smoke from its engines as they worked desperately to flee as the submarines below.

The water changed from its natural form and now fully tried to wrap around itself caused from the spinning water of Sara'. The destroyer from Russia now had its nose sticking in the air and the rear of the ship pointed toward the mouth of the queen's killer. People aboard the ship dared not jump off board into the water. The water spoke of death to the crew personnel and the people stayed aboard the large ship as long as possible, before they were forcefully made to hand over their lives.

Sara' exited her spin and floated outside of her creation. The Russian ships traveled down the deadly funnel and now so did its passengers, for they were all dead. The crew was completely dead. The whirlpool broke its prey into pieces making it easier to devour its prey. The large, broken up ship mildly spun down toward the ocean floor and the submarines were the next victim of this funnel.

The turbine engines of the submarines were no match for the strength of the funnel. The engine of the submarines pushed its exhaust into the cold water continuing its attempted escape. The funnel spun harder tugging at the submarine and sucking up its exhaust. The whirlpool was a multitasker as it finished with the ship and its crewmen and women. The whirl pool digested its prey and its contents onto the ocean floor, stirring up the sand and muck.

The funnel now grabbed the rear of the submarine and slung the large underwater vessel to the right. The submarine was spilt into two pieces, causing bubble heads to be thrown from their craft along with debris from their submarine. The ocean water was covered with much trash and pollutions from the engines from the ship and oil tanks of the submarine. The ocean water was black and hard to see through with zero visibility.

Sara' swam up toward the surface of the Bering Sea so that her children will know that a mother's worst fear is to see a child kill his or her brother or sister. The queen swam from the side of the funnel, and now broke the surface of the violent water. Sara' climbed from the water, walking toward the mouth of her created killer. All naval ships fled as fast as their engines would carry them, and all air units fled toward land from the threat of running out of fuel at sea.

Sara' stood before the killer, telling it to close its mouth as it has eaten plenty. The mouth closed and now rested some place in the deep blue sea. After the mouth of the whirlpool was shut, Sara' walked across the water toward Russia. All eyes were focused back on the queen and it was for a moment believed she was murdered from Russia's first air attack.

Walking calmly and looking in all directions, Sara' looked at all the ships in the ocean, and the fleeing planes and jets. The queen spoke softly amongst herself. "My daughter Thomas, send my children home out of their neighbor yard." The ships of the queen began to leave, and head further away from Russia heading home as instructed. The grounded planes of the queen also headed back in the air and toward the decks of the ships which carried them across the seas.

Sara' continued walking toward her now scared children of Russia. The queen closed her eyes tightly and spoke to all her ground troops telepathically, ordering them to travel back home as well. The troops of Sara' turned around in robotic form and headed home with no questions of their short touristic visit to the large iron country.

Opening back up her eyes, Sara' kept striding forward and the invading ships headed toward their country's beach. The fleeing naval ships wanted to beach themselves in order to run from Sara''s wrath. The Russians were terrified. The president of this brave country grabbed a gun from his office drawer and shot himself dead, point black in the head. The president assumed Sara' wanted to make an example of him, for his country's defiance.

Rain began to fall and Sara"s partially dried hair started to become drenched and flattened against her face. Horns sounded off from the large ships warning their crew and bystanders standing off Russia coastline of an emergency beaching of their ships. The horns were loud and people speedily ran further back from the water.

Planes flew overhead of Sara' and followed her orders.

Ships from overseas got deeper out and headed toward home. The sun had not fully set and there was plenty of light for curious people to get quality images of Sara' through their living room televisions. High-powered news cameras were responsible for most of the pictures of the beautiful being.

However, the horns of Russian naval ships continued to blow at their maximum capacity. The queen was not distracted and faced straight ahead and having much faith that the water will support her weight. Hundreds of people now fled in anticipation of the beached naval ships. The people aboard the ships appeared to want to jump from the large ships into the freezing water. People jumped into the cold water and took their chances.

Land was not far out for Sara' and the ships, so plugging into the seawater didn't have dire consequences. A loud scraping sound was heard. A naval ship had hit something under the water, making the injured ship wobble violently. Sara' remained only a short amount of distance from land, behind the approaching ships.

The injured ship was the first to hit land after being struck from something below the water. The second ship hit land also shortly after the injured ship, and other Russian ships soon followed behind. Thousands of crew personnel stood on the decks of their beached ships, staring at uncertainties.

Thousands and thousands of people standing on the coast of the beach could not fully see Sara' clearly. All the people saw was an image of a human figure walking on the ocean water. Sara' approached the rear of the ship as she held her head up at the crewmen and women who gazed upon her.

Sara' now walked between two of the beached ships and now she was fully seen by the pedestrians on the beach. People on the beach ran further back from the shoreline as the queen approached them. People aboard the naval ships looked off the side of their ships down at Sara' who walked ever so calmly.

The queen was at the midpoint of the Russian crew carriers and only had short steps left before she reached the shoreline. Crew personnel walked toward the rear of their ships, as Sara' headed for the front of their ships. Flashing lights winked at the queen from many cameras from news crews and freelance photographers. People on the beach appeared like ants fleeing from the approaching queen as their new ruler continued to walk closer toward them.

Russian police and SWAT units hid at various angles around their beach with weapons pointed at the queen. Screams were heard from many miles around on the Russian beach and the people continued to run further back as news crews captured every hysterical moment.

The queen touched the land of Russia and walked further. People on the beach stopped their fleeing once they felt it safe to make their escape temporarily. Sara' faced seas of Russians on the beach as she herself quit her motion toward the crowds. SWAT units and other Russian officers tightened their grips around their assault weapons, as they monitored Sara' from long range.

Further orders came over all radio signals from Russia, commanding that no one fire their weapon until given orders. However, every person of public service on the beach focused through the sights of their weapons. The queen stood in one place for what felt like eternity. The beach front was absent of any sound, the people appeared frightened and thought maybe if they were silent that Sara' idiotically would not notice them.

Sara' looked around at her foreign audience before delivering a message to the Russian country: "Children, don't be afraid. I love you. Children, there is a purpose for my actions. I have come to love you. Gather around, children of Russia. Your wars serve very little meaning. A day will come when you must protect yourselves.

"A more dominating male species will visit your world and decide to keep your plant for themselves. Children, we will heal from our wars and learn to love each other dearly.

"We will guard our section of the galaxy and allow our planet and the animals living amongst us, time to heal with our planet. Discipline comes at a valuable cost. A mother will die for her children and she will educate them."

After the queen finished her message, many people dropped toward the ground and cried out loudly. Sara' rose high into the sky after speaking and then vanished from Russia. News and military camera crews pointed their lenses high into the sky, following the queen. The queen moved her lips as she looked at the storm one last time. It started to rain over the Bering Sea and the Russian citizens rose their wet faces from the ground and up into the rainy sky.

The queen was long gone and the people of this country stand around unsure of what to think or do next. Far out at sea, the ships from over the Atlantic were starting to disappear over the horizon, and neighbors were leaving their neighbor's yard.

NUMBERS!

Numbers meant everything when domination took its place moving past the elite. Sara' destroyed all members of the American government, destroying their country's structural form. America was taken over and now held their head low with shame! The American flag color now was entirely black except for six purple colored stars, located on the upper right corner of the flag. The black garment hung sideways as the original American flag had once remained.

Sara' allowed Ms. Thomas to partner beside her. Ms. Thomas stood five feet seven inches. However, Sara' was a giant compared to Ms. Thomas, by standing six feet even inches. Numbers meant everything! Sara' took control of the middle parts of the world, and uses the United States of America as a home base. The planet earth glowed fire red looking at the planet from outer space.

People of earth thought and believed that a day such as this one would and could never happen. However, numbers will and could destroy anything and for Sara' to dominate the planet earth was not hard for the new queen to do. The country of Russia put up a tremendous battle but the opposition's numbers were just too great for the large and brave country.

After Russia's loss to Sara', many uninvaded countries began to give up and surrender voluntarily. The countries of China, Japan, Australia, Ireland, Poland, and many more countries around the planet gave up and surrendered to the numbers of Sara' Leon. The humanoid woman from the planet Adamen fully took over planet earth, and now sought control of solar systems and any possible planet from invading her new home.

The queen Sara' Leon loved earth and she was willing to give up her own life before she would allow anything, person or any humanoid being, to hurt this world. Meanwhile Sara' sent home all her troops from all countries and back to their own territories. Also women around the world in second and third world countries were being educated from missionaries of the queen of earth through special programs constructed from members of Sara''s technology groups.

Sara' also repaired broken governments in several countries around the world, and she gave governments to several small towns and villages inside of third world countries so that everyone around the planet could receive education for the purpose of making the planet earth ready for all un-expectedness.

Imagine a world with only a few strong areas and not a world that could fully protect itself. Sara' felt that certain countries around the world only wanted to defeat members of their fellow country man. Sara' felt that the earth's males were not equipped to protect himself from threats from outside their solar system.

Earth will never be the same again for men around the world. A new start took place and women were now dominant over men. Sara' sat behind the scenes and controlled her world, and she was the only member of her secret society. Ms. Thomas, oversaw all operations of anything of importance. There have been a chain of order and command before things of concern would reach the queen.

Satellite television and radio broadcast was released over airwaves of countries giving up any resistance toward not accepting the queen's law and order. The remaining countries refused to put their countries at stake by allowing Sara"s numbers to enter the land of their forefathers and destroy precious lives and blood lines of the people of their country.

A battle of worlds soon will take place and earth will only have twenty-four months to prepare themselves. Sara' understood that a time of preparedness was at hand.